Leo was born and raised in Rosemead, California. Growing up, he was artistically inclined in both drawing and written literature and during high school, decided he preferred writing.

Leo

THE RIGHT OATH

AUSTIN MACAULEY PUBLISHERS
LONDON * CAMBRIDGE * NEW YORK * SHARJAH

Copyright © Leo 2025

All rights reserved. No part of this publication may be reproduced, distributed, or transmitted in any form or by any means, including photocopying, recording, or other electronic or mechanical methods, without the prior written permission of the publisher, except in the case of brief quotations embodied in critical reviews and certain other noncommercial uses permitted by copyright law. For permission requests, write to the publisher.

Any person who commits any unauthorized act in relation to this publication may be liable to criminal prosecution and civil claims for damages.

This is a work of fiction. Names, characters, businesses, places, events, locales, and incidents are either the products of the author's imagination or used in a fictitious manner. Any resemblance to actual persons, living or dead, or actual events is purely coincidental.

Ordering Information:
Quantity sales: special discounts are available on quantity purchases by corporations, associations, and others. For details, contact the publisher at the address below.

Publisher's Cataloging-in-Publication data
Leo
The Right Oath

ISBN 9781645756897 (Paperback)
ISBN 9781645756903 (Hardback)
ISBN 9781645756910 (ePub e-book)

Library of Congress Control Number: 2024901055

www.austinmacauley.com/us

First Published 2025
Austin Macauley Publishers LLC
40 Wall Street, 33rd Floor, Suite 3302
New York, NY 10005
USA

+1 (646) 5125767

Trent Hertzog, you were the first guy to have ever read the story in its beginning phase back out there in the gulf, for that I thank you brother.

Chapter 1
The Baseline

I wish I could say I remember how good life was when I came back to Long Beach, California. I wish I could say how peaceful a life I was living before I entered eighth grade. A year later and I am still suffering from what I could only describe as my own self-inflicted karma. And recently, it's only gotten worse. And I'm only fifteen years old. A kid shouldn't be dealing with what I have on my plate.

I keep having this recurring nightmare, one where I'm dressed semi-formally, blue shirt, black vest and slacks. My black hair had been ruffled and messy, clearly from a night of partying hard. And with me was a girl dressed in a breathtaking backless, ocean blue dress. She had no shoes on, just her black linen stockings, and we were in the foyer of a home I was very familiar with. Every time I have had this dream, she'd walk ahead of me and always say the same damn phrase, like on repeat. Time after time, without anything new.

"Gabe, tonight was wonderful," she'd say. "I loved everything about it. I'm glad we're with each other."

And I'd stare at her back, silently. But not without action. I could see the retractable blade that was hidden under the sleeve on my right arm, as it slowly descended with slight clicks and hisses. I want so desperately to shout out to her, "watch out!" but I can't do anything but watch. I watched as once the blade was fully extended, I approached her from behind and spun her about quickly into my arms. I had been embracing her with my left, like a lover would, but the blade was stabbing her through the chest. Straight clean through her heart.

The shocked, pained expression on her face, the near flawless tan skin, the wavy brown hair with highlights of lighter shades, and the dinner plate wide rustic brown eyes of horror, could barely believe who just killed her without batting an eye was nigh erasable from my sight or memory. It was so heavily ingrained into my mind, the memory may as well have had its own memory, just to remind and spite me all at once. Reminding me that I was a murderer, I was also a traitor. On two counts.

Thankfully, the nightmare this time ended abruptly after I stabbed her, but whether the nightmare itself continued from that point on wouldn't have done me any favors.

I shot straight up, yelling in anguish in my room. Sweat drenched my white tank top from the nightmare I had had the displeasure of enduring. My bed, or bedding so to speak, was quite literally the floor plus blankets and a pillow. It was a choice I made based on the belief I didn't deserve a real bed.

The darkness in my room was the only other companion I had, save for the moonlight from the window and the fluorescent light that bled slightly from the small crack underneath my door. It was a sign my actual physical companion had awoken. More than likely coming in response to my anguished yell.

The door burst open, but I paid no mind to the presence at the door. All I allowed my vision to catch were the small, feminine bare feet that belonged to my housemate.

"Gabriel, are you alright?" I heard her smooth, concerned voice call to me as I sat on my bedding. "I heard you yell from my room. Was it another—"

"It was just another nightmare, Raven," I said, agitated, not just from the dream, but from Raven's presence itself. "Don't worry about it. Just go back to bed."

I imagine she must've felt hurt when I didn't see her move immediately after my commands. It only served to annoy me more. Don't misunderstand, I didn't hate her, rather it was what she represented that set me off even more. To me, she was my greatest reminder of who I was and what I'd done. I refused to even meet her gaze. And all she'd done was let me do as I please. She didn't even know what I'd been seeing in my dreams. It sickened me how Raven just took it all in stride these last couple of weeks we'd started living together. Ever since my best friend, my girlfriend, died.

It was funny how Raven suddenly came into my life. Told me it was thanks to Elouise and her genius-level intellect behind biotechnology that saved her life from a terminal disease that had already robbed her of her arms and legs. Her body wouldn't have been long after, were it not for Elouise.

And who exactly was this Elouise that I'd been mentioning? That would be my girlfriend. She and I grew up living only a couple of houses down the street. What made her more special than anyone else I'd known was just how crazy smart she was. Remember how I mentioned she was a genius? Well, she maintained and continuously improved on crazy technological designs to the point she was decades beyond anyone else's capacity to understand. What only served to enable her creations and future projects had been the fact her family were business giants. Their wealth fueled her creations. In turn, she allowed some of her more sensible and simpler creations on the market.

Of all the things for her to specialize in, she wanted to create better prosthetic limbs for people with disabilities. Even going so far as to learn how to perform the surgical procedures to personally see to it that the cybernetic implants were applied properly. She first practiced on animals, dogs, elephants, even birds. But the first person she ever worked on, as far as I knew, was me.

I lost my arm in an explosion that killed my family in our new home. When Elouise took me in, she gave me a new arm. One year later though, she was killed in a car accident, as the official story anyways. That was when Raven showed up, explaining her story to me and the others that had been there. But while the others chose to accept and welcome the anomaly that was Raven Loecroft, I knew better.

Raven remained in the doorway, continuing to accept my disregard for her.

"Are you sure you don't need anything? I can get you a glass of water or—"

"Raven!" I shouted at her. "I said, go back to bed. It's the dead of night. We have school in the morning."

"Ah… Alright…" Raven said, so sullen and suppressed.

She didn't make another sound as she closed the door behind her and left. I laid back onto my bedding and stared directly up at the ceiling, as if to find something worthwhile to think of. Something to take my mind off everything about the dream, about Raven, and how my life would soon go right back into the "norm".

I didn't have a say in that matter, so I slowly drifted back quietly to sleep.

With the morning came an internal alarm in my head, thanks to a cybernetic implant Elouise put in me to work with the arm she gave me. I used it more often these days because I'd not been sleeping well and I couldn't trust myself to wake up on account of my nightmares.

My morning routine was simple enough, wake up, wash up, shake off the grogginess and dress up. A simple dark shirt, deep blue jeans and black sneakers and a grey jacket to cover up my jet-black metal right arm.

I cared little for what Raven had to wear. So long as she got ready before I did, I was fine. It was only six-thirty, fifteen minutes before the bus showed up to take us to school. I grabbed my backpack, slinging it on a single shoulder and made my way down from the second floor of my home. I wasted no time going for the door, expecting Raven to follow suit.

"Gabriel! I've made breakfast, if you want some," Raven announced behind me. It was practically needless.

I gave her my back, but I at least acknowledged her intentions.

"I don't want it, Raven," I said, loudly, clearly and coldly. "You're free to eat some yourself if you haven't already."

"I... Already had some to satisfy what my body needs..." Raven said cautiously. I still refused to face her.

I already began turning the knob on the door to head out, fully expecting Raven to understand I had no intention of staying any second longer.

"Gabriel," Raven called to me, causing me to stop in my stride after opening the door. "If there's something wrong, you can talk to me. I promised Elouise I'd help you if something were to happen to her."

Lies.

"But if you can't bring yourself to tell me anything, I can't help."

It was all lies.

"So please, just let me know, okay?"

I let loose a heavy sigh, having become exhausted by Raven's words that were more rotten than she knew. Everything she said held no weight, and she'd never know why, nor did she have any idea that they were. As far as she knew, all I'd been was distant, introverted and standoffish. If anything, I was being outright contemptuous of her very being. But I couldn't blame her.

"Let's just go already," I said outright, trying to disregard her words. "You can save what's left when we come back home for later. I'd rather not miss the bus."

Raven followed after me like a duckling and we both headed down the street toward the bus stop where we found Jude and Sena together, just as they had been before. Jude was pretty much my second best friend after Elouise, and Sena, his girlfriend, was close with us all as well. Both of them were like your typical high school jock and pretty girl couple. Except Jude was more stand-up and humble than most and Sena was a sweetheart and was a genuine good-natured person.

These days, they were more worried about me than usual. I mean before, when I lost my family, they tried to keep me in good spirits as I had only one arm and no family left. I was one of those depressed kids who thought there was nothing left anymore. But they were always trying, and I was thankful for that. Then again, it was really Elouise that gave me new purpose in life. Now that she was gone, they were probably worried that I would slump back into worse straits again.

It wasn't like I would ever consider just ending my life. No, that'd insult Elouise's memory and everything she'd done for me. Although, I wouldn't exactly say I wouldn't welcome death. It certainly be the least I deserve after what I've done. And they had no idea what I've been doing.

"You look like hell, man," Jude said jokingly, giving me a concerned look with his smirk. "You still having trouble sleeping?"

I scoffed and gave a wry grin.

"Gee, was it that obvious?" I sarcastically quipped. "Hey Sena, good morning."

"Good morning to you too, though I gotta agree with Jude. You look like you're still having trouble sleeping," Sena said with a worrisome look.

"I'll be fine, I promise," I said quickly to dismiss their concerns.

"Based on what I've seen, Gabriel, it hasn't gotten any better," Raven interjected like she was magically a psychologist. "At the rate you're going, you should try to consider—"

"I don't remember asking for your opinion, Raven!" I shouted angrily, which served to surprise Jude and Sena as well as catching the attention of other students around us.

I grew increasingly embarrassed and agitated that I let myself lose my cool in front of everyone. I clawed at the hair on my head with my right hand furiously, mentally berating myself for having acted out.

"Gabe, you sure you're okay?" Jude asked. "I know it's been a couple weeks since the accident, but, if you're not handling it well—"

"Can we not?" I begged with a sharp tongue, catching Jude off-guard. "Look, I'm sorry about that, I'd rather not talk about it, okay?"

Jude and Sena nodded, reluctantly so but willing to grant me some peace of mind. As for Raven… I didn't think I needed to beat the dead horse anymore to let you know I really didn't care to even bat an eye at her. Unfortunately, the remainder of the time we spent together until we got to school was spent in awkward silence thanks to my outburst. At that point though, it was a blessing. Nothing said at all meant I didn't have to deal with the skeletons in my closet. I can just focus on what school had to offer.

Wherein only offered the same, monotonous schedule of classes, boring lectures that I could simply learn in mere minutes through my ability to access any information in cyberspace with my arm. It was like cheating, but no one knew any better. The worst part wasn't the bore that was schoolwork and lectures, or the fact that the school staff all knew who I was and what I did, it was the fact in every single damn class, Raven was always there.

Never mind the fact my handler managed to manipulate the school district I was in to pretty much have them acknowledge, and accept, I would sometimes disappear for days at a time. Even that I was guaranteed a high school diploma no matter what happened…

And at the end of every class, this message would pop up in my heads-up display from my right eye: "No official word yet from Control. We're to continue our day as normal." I could be convinced it was automated, but I just knew it was always done consciously by Raven. That was her role for me. My "partner", gifted to me by the people I worked for.

Lunch was no different today than most. We met up with Jude and Sena, we hung out, talked a little bit, and then we went our separate ways. Nothing new, nothing different. I liked it that way, and I almost wished it never would end. I wished for a lot of things lately. But wishing wouldn't get me anywhere. I mean, Elouise didn't wish for genius-level intellect. She didn't wish to be preyed upon by rival tech giants that wanted to use her mind for their own personal gain. She didn't wish to die by a car accident. I didn't wish to get stuck in a life where I always held a trigger.

My school day, and week, ended as normally as could be for any sophomore in high school. However, today instead of taking the bus home with Jude and Sena, I decided to take a walk elsewhere. Once I said goodbye to them, I headed off on my own down the streets and began to simply wander, aimlessly.

Where I was at in my life, who could really tell me what to do? I had no parents, I had no one at home who I could call my legal guardian. Those people were Elouise's parents, and they were always busy travelling. Too busy to stay at home for a day. Too busy for Elouise's sake. Most kids my age would think they'd have it made.

I sure as hell didn't.

I kept wandering about until I found myself in downtown area. All sorts of noises assaulted me, my right eye, capable of scanning just about anything and collect information within moments had been flooding my head with all manner of data. It wasn't automatic, I was intentionally doing it. Anything to take my mind off my own troubles. Speaking of troubles…

"How long are you going to kccp following me, Raven?" I asked without turning as I walked down the street.

"I can't leave you alone, Gabriel," Raven said plainly. "I'm not allowed to."

"Is it because of your promise? Or is it because Jackson ordered it?"

"You know why."

"Do I? Gee, I must know everything off the top of my freaking head then! Hey, did you know you can book a trip to Catalina from Long Beach? Or hey, did you know the sports arena here has one of the artist Robert Wyland's Whaling Walls there?"

The entire time I'd been going off, I'd been walking along, probably drawing all manner of attention from people around. I could care less what they thought. It was Friday evening. I didn't care what I did, or where I went. The only time I stopped walking was at a crosswalk.

"Gabriel, please," Raven begged tenderly. "I just want to help you, but—"

"I heard you the first time, and the time after that too," I said angrily. "And I. Don't. Care."

"But…"

"Raven, you can go home without me, I can find my way home easy." I commanded outright, just as the crosswalk sign light up to allow pedestrians to cross. "You want to help me? You can start by leaving me alone."

I continued my wandering, hoping that Raven would have obeyed my commands and left to go home. She'd make it back faster than me anyways if she really wanted to. Raven had that capacity.

You don't have to be alone the rest of your life, Gabriel.

Goddamn soulless…It's my choice, Raven. Stay out of my head.

I get it. I'm a stranger in your life. I'm not Elouise, I can't replace her.

You're damn right you can't.

But that doesn't mean I can't be to you what she was.

Infuriated, I spun about, brushing past others that had been behind me, and found Raven in my sights. First time in a while that I had actually laid eyes on her, but only the lower half. I still refused to look her in the face. So in the middle of the sidewalk, people saw a young boy staring low toward the ground at a girl who was almost my height.

"Don't get ahead of yourself, you empty shell!" I shouted at the top of my lungs, completely void of any care about outward appearances. "You think of all these things you believe you can do, but you'll never be able to! You're just a replacement part! A cog in the machine! To me, you're about as replaceable as a wheel on a car!"

"And here I am, still," Raven said almost devoid of emotion.

I growled in frustration, because that simple statement had pointed out that despite how much I made sense, Raven was ultimately what replaced Elouise. And I still hadn't tossed her aside.

"Hey kid, is everything alright here?" Someone much older came up behind me and placed a hand on my shoulder.

I heard other murmurs behind him as well. Some of them sounded like high school students form the way they talked. A lot of their comments mentioned how much of a terrible boyfriend I was being or how Raven should just leave me in the dust and find someone else. All misconceptions. Terrible, misguided ideas.

I turned around and met with some guy who had about a few inches on me, and maybe an extra fifty pounds of muscle. I was five-ten, so he was pretty tall. Looked like a decent kind of guy too, even with his gaggle of friends behind him.

"Everything is fine," I said gruffly. "Just stay out of my business."

He cocked an eye at me, as if he was impressed that someone younger than him was taking such an attitude with him despite how polite he was being. Oh please, do me a favor and just walk. I'm not in a peaceful mood tonight. I turned away from him, resuming my previous standoff with Raven, though now it was a silent chatter of instant messages inside my head.

"Hey, kid, no need to be so aggressive," the guy behind me continued. And then he grabbed my arm.

You're not going to leave are you? I asked Raven while staring down at her denim-covered legs.

"Look, it's probably for the best if you just leave the girl alone, alright? Hey, you there, why don't you hang out with us? We're better company than this little fireball here."

I told you before, I promised Elouise I'd help you.

Fine then.

"She's not going anywhere with you..." I muttered angrily.

"And you think I'm going to leave her here with you? Get real, kid, this isn't some cartoon where you act all dark and broody—"

The cool guy didn't get a chance to finish his statement because I had whipped around and roundhouse kicked him in the head. I learned a lot over a single year. Like aiming for a guaranteed knockout blow on a human head. I stood in a fighting stance, fists clenched into powerful battering tools, legs spread for a stable and strong pose. People around us where shocked, unable to stop staring as they walked. The sap who was on the floor hadn't moved a muscle. I glared back at his friends who were all processing what just happened.

I stood my ground, but gave them all a smirk, inviting them to get some payback. Immediately, two of the four guys charged at me. But one of them was met with a flying kick into his gut by Raven, having taken a running start once they charged. The other guy grabbed me, but I countered him by lowering my center of gravity, throwing him over my head and onto his back. A single snap of my right arm rendered him unconscious.

When I looked up, I saw the back of Raven's long, black hair. She was in her own fighting stance against the remainder of the group. but the two other guys and the two girls that were with them had cowered and ran. Nobody else wanted to intervene. Nobody had the guts to. One look at the guys on the floor, unconscious and unmoving had explicitly stated "Do not even try." The worst part of this all: Raven and I would get off scot-free from local law enforcement. But that didn't mean we wouldn't face consequences.

Satisfied? Raven asked.

No. But I feel better.

You know we'll have to report this to Control?

I. Don't. Care.

I. Don't. Care.

Chapter 2
Reality of the Situation

Another nightmare, except this time, it was different. I was in a certain particular warehouse. What was once empty was now bustling with workers handling all sorts of machinery and equipment. But it closely resembled a laboratory. And I was standing right before an old man of whom I could only have described as a Santa Claus dressed in a lab coat. His name was Alexander, but as far as I knew, his name was just a cover. He wasn't a man who wanted to be found, so it surprised me that Jackson, my handler, had been there with him, standing next to him looking like a dumb Agent Smith knockoff. One with a dumbass, smug smile, slicked back blonde hair and equally stupid sunglasses that he never once taken off in the time I've known him.

Alexander had played a critical role in my life just with one single phone call. It was thanks to him managing to contact me and sending me to a mall did I acquire a vital piece of technology that helped boost my arm's capabilities to be limitless without risk. All thanks to what he called the "chaos engine", a small energy reactor that my arm assimilated into itself on contact. It provided it the power it needed to activate the overdrive feature on it without it killing me in the process.

I thought I'd never hear from him again, much less see. Even when Jackson told me after he learned of my interaction that he wanted to know if I ever met with him so he himself could. It was clear he had found Alexander his own way. Not that he would ever tell me. It was always a need to know basis with him. And I didn't need to know.

But in that dream, that memory of me meeting with both of them had been about a potential solution to the problem that had been the reason why I'd been working for Jackson. The various tech groups that had targeted Elouise had been the major reason why I was dead set on protecting Elouise at any cost. If only I knew what that mindset really meant for us.

I was excited to hear Jackson giving me a small ray of hope that at last, she and I would finally be able to live our lives normally, like most teenagers in high school. But then came the words that I dreaded hearing.

"Elouise Gaines has to die," Jackson had proclaimed with such a deadly serious tone, I was convinced his laidback attitude was a facade for his true cold, heartless soul.

I had stared pale-faced at the both of them. I was unable to fully comprehend what Jackson had stated. But that's where the dream came to a sudden end. I was shaken awake by Raven who'd been sitting beside me. I awoke groggily, the sight of the cargo hold of the flying steel trap of the plane we'd been riding in had graced my vision gradually as my eyes adjusted to the dim red lighting in the bay.

Once I lowered my head, I took in the sight of my own tactical clothing and combat boots. It served as a grim, depressing reminder I was back to the "norm" of my life. A boy soldier who swore to protect the one thing that mattered most... Or at least I used to. Nowadays, I wasn't sure why I continued if only to comply with Jackson's demands for further guaranteed safety.

Maybe I was hoping one day I'd get what I deserved.

Raven's hand had still been resting on my shoulder from having woken me up. I didn't look at her directly, but I could see the heavy pants she were that were bloused above the knee, exposing the skin of her bare legs and feet. She also had on a specifically designed combat vest and shirt that left much of her lower arms exposed. There'd been a reason for that, but for the time being, you could imagine she looked like some sort of model with a military inspiration.

Well, if looks could kill...

"What's goin' on...?" I asked sleepily.

"We're about thirty minutes from the drop zone, and... You were stirring in your sleep," Raven said gently. "Another nightmare?"

I sighed, resigned to my fate. After all, we were stuck in a plan together. I couldn't run away from her, and ignoring her had already proven futile.

"Yeah... 'Nother nightmare..."

To clear up confusion as to what was really happening, it was well into Sunday, afternoon over the continent of Africa. More than likely over the Congo. Raven and I had been on a mission, but in a way it was like a punishment. The other day when I fought those random guys in the street hadn't gone without notice by Jackson and gave me and Raven a scathing earful about being reckless and how his resources are not to be wasted on civilians when not on mission. As such, our mission that we started Saturday, was to go into the Congo, seek out a particular warlord and eliminate him by any means necessary.

"Being daytime might affect our mission progress," Raven noted. "A stealth-based approach may not be the best tactic for—"

"I don't care what tactic we use," I aggressively said. "We've got the green light to do whatever it takes to get the job done. And the sooner we get it done, sooner we go home... Maybe I can actually sleep for once..."

"Mmn... Understood," Raven said defeated.

It might've been Sunday, but school didn't matter so long as I kept my end of the bargain. But I would love it if I could miss school and sleep for a day. That'd be a lovely privilege.

Sometime later, the pilot spoke through a speaker in the cargo hold, alerting me and Raven we were ten minutes out, telling us to get ready. As such, Raven and I unbuckled ourselves and headed to the rear of the plane. It'd been completely empty save for us. We stood by at the edge of the cargo bay door hinge, gripping onto the side for support. Raven had been behind me, ready to go as I'd been.

I'd worn the same face as I always did on these jobs: Emotionless, stone cold and calculating. Out on these missions, there was no room for anything that could distract me... Even my nightmares.

"Gabriel," Raven called from behind me. "If there's something bothering you—"

"Don't," I scathingly said. "If you think my nightmares are going to get in the way, Raven, then you're sorely misjudging me."

"I… I just want to make sure you'll be fine; that you won't be distracted," Raven continued.

Hmph, think about who you're talking to, you puppet… I've been at this for over a year now. I'm not the same naive brat I started out as.

"Five minutes, kiddos!" the pilot announced. The alarm blared out in the plane as the door slowly opened. Air rushed about from the shift in air pressure, creating a vortex of air that tried to suck us out. But we were well anchored to the plane's interior. The most the wind did was toss our hair. Outside, I could see the vast sky, and the vast Congo below. Time to make final preps, starting with my radio linkup with Raven. It would keep us in the loop, allowing us to see what the other did.

Link established. Signal holding at one hundred percent, Gabriel.

Good. You have our target's identity?

Confirmed. I've also our landing site, sending data to your HUD.

Received. Sixty seconds to jump. Standby.

When the time came, the pilot alerted us as our signal to go, and I took the first leap into the whistling air. All without a parachute. It was the first time I've done this, but I had complete faith my partner knew what to do.

I was in a full dive, my right eye kept open as its artificial nature meant it wasn't subject to the blistering wind that met me in my dive. As such, I kept a constant lock on the target location to land.

It didn't take long for Raven to catch me in full dive from behind. I felt latches grasping me around my chest and waist.

I'm connected to you, Gabriel.

Good. Take us in, Raven.

Our descent began to slow to a more manageable speed. Not only that, but we began to level out and began falling feet first. I kept my focus down to the forest below, directly at the clearing that was meant for both our insertion and escape. The deafening sound of the air was lessened and with the lessened intensity of the rushing air, I was able to keep both eyes open. But with the lack of rushing air, came a new noise. The one I was expecting, the thrust of jets that slowed our descent.

Raven's legs had transformed fully into jet constructs. Powerful enough to send her flying at mach one, so carrying us both and providing a slow controlled descent was a cinch for her. Once we'd gotten within five feet of landing, I gave the mental order through our private channel to drop me. I landed into a roll to lessen the effect of gravity. Once back on my feet, I caught a glimpse of Raven's cybernetic body. Her lower legs and arms had been completely transformed into segmented, black steel armored forms. Her fingers, clawed, her legs expanded slightly from the usage of her leg jets. In addition her back was exposed, revealing portions of her upper back had been cybernetically altered as well with black armored plates creating an extra set of jets to provide further thrust.

That being said, all I suffered to see of Raven had been her back. Once she transformed her lower legs into actual armored feet, she let herself down with her back jets. When she began to turn and face me, I lowered my gaze to the dirt once more and moved past her so I could look into the forest line, using my data to find the most direct route to our target.

Gabriel, I've the most direct route to our target, sixty kilometers out. I can get us there quickly without any problem.

By land I would imagine? Last thing I'd want to do is telegraph our arrival anymore.

Of course. But we'll have to stop before we reach the warlord's compound. If we intend to catch them by surprise.

Perfect. I wish you were more like this, Raven. Less emotional baggage and more practical in action.

Says you, the one who seems to have the most between us.

Well. Played. I cursed myself mentally. I made no waste in turning about and finding Raven's back already present to me, beholding to me a harness constructed from her back cybernetic armor, with footrests extending away from her to make a pseudo seat for me. I placed myself onto her back with my own, making myself look like a backpack. She'd already re-purposed her legs into a reversed form so she could lean forward with my weight on her back while balancing herself. Soon, we began moving at a brisk pace, one that matched an automobile meant for extreme off-road. Another of her constructs.

Her feet became wheels with powerful engines within her calves. Powerful as they were, the engines only slightly hummed like a small electrical motor that had been muffled by the exterior armor. The only other noises that welcomed me as we plowed through the forest were the undergrowth, branches and other foliage that Raven simply ran over. It didn't take us long, maybe less than twenty minutes before we slowed to a stop. Once I hopped off I walked quickly past Raven and observed what lay ahead.

A large compound that'd been teeming with militia. And many of them looked young, younger than me even. More child soldiers. Though in comparison, I had to have been far worse than any of them, just based on history alone. More a mark of shame than pride. Nothing about my history screams honorable, not even close to respectable. These people? These kids? They may have been forced into this life for other reasons. I chose this.

Raven, find a good overlook of the base. I'll make the approach to it and make my way to the target. From my eye's scans, he's just casually watching sports on his television. Once I deal with him, move in to extract me and we'll head back to the landing site for retrieval.

Understood, I'll provide support when needed.

Raven zipped off and away, leaving me all by my lonesome.

I remembered my first jobs. They were always alone. I had no one else accompanying me, except the voice of that jackass, Jackson. Speaking of…

I flexed my exposed right arm, the segmented steel with a small blue core in the palm expanded and created a communicator that would neatly wrap around my ear. I gently placed it to my head and began contacting Jackson, also known as…

"Control, Raven and I have made it to the target location and are commencing operations," I said plainly over the communicator. I waited for a minute, but with no answer I grew increasingly agitated. "Control... Are you even awake...?"

No answer.

"Control?"

"Ah, Wha—Oh Gabe! Good afternoon I imagine!" Jackson said in his pious, happy-go-lucky self.

"Control... Wake the hell up already and confirm my previous report!" I said angrily and impatiently.

"Ah, why do you have to yell in my ear half the time you're working? It's like our roles are reversed, considering what happened Friday, Gabriel."

I growled in response, but didn't respond.

"But of course, I've you and Raven on my feed and can confirm you're most definitely conducting operations as planned!"

Great. That was all the talk I needed to do with him for now.

"I'll contact you again once our objective has been completed."

With that I removed the communicator and re-assimilated the device back into my arm. This thing was quite the piece of work. Elouise's design for it was one of the major reasons why the rival groups against her family wanted her. Making a robotic arm that functioned like a human one was one thing, but she took it one step further.

She comprised the entire thing out of her own specially designed nanomachines. Completely autonomous and can specialize themselves to suit whatever need was required, they were even self-repairing and auto maintained themselves. To say they acted like a cell would for a real human arm, but better, the machines could repurpose themselves on a whim. Combined with my other implants that Elouise put in me, my arm had the ability to reform and become any weapon I wanted, and the basis for those weapons came from the data collected from my right eye.

That was right, I'd the power to scan technology of any kind and then use my arm to copy, recreate and create anything I wished. Firearms were just a basic trick. But forget the necessity for gunpowder, my firearms used electromagnetics. That meant all my firearms were essentially railguns.

Devastating, I knew, but I learned how to use them responsibly and not recklessly. I was not just a kid with weapons of mass destruction.

I moved quickly on foot, making it closer to their fence that spanned the entirety of their compound. From my HUD, I made several watch towers with their own armed watchmen, some of them were provided by Raven from her own vantage point. In addition, there'd been plenty of roving guards. I had to remember they weren't just soldiers... They'd been like me.

And so, I made my move. I didn't waste much time analyzing my path to the target. I moved on instinct, from a year's worth of constant combat and infiltration experience and my own cybernetically enhanced reflexes and equipment.

Any obstacle, or any soldier that may have become a threat was silenced by Raven with her own variation of firearms she had access to, just like I did. But where I only had an arm and a small array of optical enhancements through my right eye, she had arms, back, legs and head. She was superior to me in every way, and she was to act as support. Hilarious. Elouise would hate me if she knew exactly what I'd been doing.

I made my way into the warlord's building he'd been in, and quickly made my way to his closed room. With an x-ray scan from my right eye, I made sure he wasn't alerted and staying still in his chair. With precise aiming with my arm, I transformed it into a powerful rifle with all manner of whirs, clinks and clanks. With a low hum, the rifle precharged itself. With my will alone, I aimed, fully charged, and fired through the wall and the chest of the warlord behind it.

Easy. Simple. Now was time to run. The shot was easy for anyone within earshot to have heard, after all, a fully charged electromagnetic bullet fired that broke the sound barrier would definitely make some noise. But it's what I wanted. Noise to the warlords exact location, to draw in soldiers to thin out the potential threats that I would meet in my escape.

I quickly made for the nearest window and smashed through it. But I didn't fall to the ground. I repurposed my arm to fire a grapnel hook into the wall and pulled myself toward it. I climbed up with my arm to the roof and made my way toward the end of it, heading for the exit of the compound. I could hear the cries of soldiers below, mourning their warlord, and scurrying about to find the assailant responsible for his death.

At the edge of the building, I saw the canopy of a truck below, so I jumped for it. I rolled over the canopy and landed on the ground next to the truck. Right near some soldiers that had been running past but had seen my leap. I met their astonished and furious faces with my cold and emotionless stare. In the next moment, Raven had bowled them over with her fists shooting straight into their backs, propelled at full force on her motor legs. She spun about, forming the harness from before.

But my eyes were subjected to a brief glimpse of her face, much of her mouth and cheeks covered in black metal plating and dark brown eyes that stared down anyone with just as equal cold and mercilessness as my own did. I hurried and strapped myself in, transforming my arm into an auto rifle in the event we are followed.

Raven zoomed off through the exit of the compound and into the forest, heading off to the landing site.

I've taken the liberty of disabling their trucks and any other vehicle capable of following.

That makes things simpler for us, I'll make contact with Control for extract.

I've done that as well. They'll be at the site within a few minutes.

Huh… This job was simple, but I never thought having someone like Raven would make this like taking candy from a baby. We were in and out in less than thirty minutes. A new personal best. I'd would be home in no time, home to see…

Oh right… I'd almost forgotten… I'm not going back home to anyone anymore…

I remember… coming back home… Elouise would be waiting, like the housewife welcoming her husband from war. Except I was constantly leaving and then coming back. Sometimes I'd be gone for a couple days. Sometimes almost a week. It was difficult for her as it was for me. Elouise was always mentally tough, but this life nearly crushed her and me all at once, but we'd somehow managed to make it work... Then she died.

And now I was stuck with a girl who made a promise that was about as empty as her very existence.

I could think of happier thoughts. For one, I knew at least Jude and Sena would never have been involved in this life. Two: I was glad they had normal lives, and not cybernetically enhanced like Raven and I. Between me and her, I knew of only one other person who'd had cybernetics in their body. And unofficially, she was dead too.

So, I guess I could go home and sleep...

Chapter 3
The Machine Trapping the Soul

Over the days that passed into the holiday season, I'd hoped Jackson would lessen the frequency of the jobs he put me and Raven up to, but I guess our first job together had impressed him greatly, because he had us do at least a dozen more before Christmas rolled around. As frequent as they were, we finished them even faster than I would have by myself. Thankfully, he saw fit to give me and Raven time off, if just for Christmas time.

And riding up to that point, Raven had always been as she always had: worrying over me in all of her very persistent ways. The funny thing was, it was working. I found myself slowly accepting her presence more and more, and no longer responding in aggressive bursts. I knew she was only doing as she felt was right, and I couldn't blame her for wanting to help me. But I still refused to look her in the eyes.

It was Christmas Eve, and I found myself just lazing on the couch, watching television, passing the time until something would happen. Raven had been beside herself at the kitchen table not far from the living room was. She was doing her homework over the vacation, of which I didn't completely understand why she'd do it considering our circumstances. Then again, I'd already did my own. Funny right? A free pass through the basic education system and I still do homework. Well, Elouise ingrained it into my head from even before that it's better to do the work yourself than rely on my arm's capabilities. As smart as she was, she preferred to stay in the standard system of schooling, if just to be around me, Jude and Sena.

One thing was for sure, Elouise was as strange as she was smart... And today happened to be the day she gave me my new arm...

I gave you that arm, because I trust you. I believe you'll use it for the best.

The remote in my hand was suddenly jerked full speed right into the TV screen, shattering the glass like a cannon ball. My right arm had been fully extended, having just launched the remote.

I stared in shock and awe that I just did that. Had my own mental state deteriorated to a point a single memory like that would just set me off like a powder keg? I grew increasingly furious, my rage seething through my mouth like hot fire as I trembled within myself while my vision slowly blurred.

But that fire was quickly put out when I felt the unmistakable warmth of Raven's body suddenly clasp itself to mine. My vision cleared up, and I could see the top of her head as she held me tight, trying to offer me comfort.

"Gabriel, it's okay," she desperately said to calm me down. "I know it must be hard for you today. Without Elouise."

You don't freaking... Say...

My rage was slowly subsiding, realizing the kind warmhearted gesture that Raven was really offering.

"It's all okay. If you want to do anything, just talk to me," Raven pleaded, as if to redirect my fury from other inanimate objects. "I'm here for you."

It was a strange thing, and an experience, for my right arm to be trembling a I slowly brought my arms around Raven. Yeah, that's right, the artificial right arm that was supposed to act as one, completely comprised of otherwise unfeeling machines, was practically reacting as my real arm would in this situation. The hesitation, the fear and the unease. The arm was being more human than I was… Or maybe, it was reminding me I was human.

I fully embraced Raven, treating her like the life preserver she wanted to become for me. I didn't say a word, and just simply took advantage of the moment for myself. I allowed myself to slightly sob into Raven's shoulder as she placed her hands onto my back, gently patting me while I quietly sobbed.

"I know I cannot ever replace her, but I told you, didn't I? I want to help you. I made her a promise I would."

"Just shut up and let me cry in peace, yeah?" I said, slightly aggressive, but more playfully irritated at Raven for constantly reminding me of her purpose in life.

She giggled from the response, obviously taking it all in stride, but seemingly much happier now that I'd finally taken the first step toward opening up to her, well, that's what I'd go as far to guess. I could never tell her the truth. It was an impossibility. Doing that could ruin the very measures that Elouise's parents, Jackson and I have taken to ensure she'd never be targeted ever again.

That was my second greatest sin. My second count of treason to Elouise.

My first? That took me back to the night of homecoming…

I was still a mess back then. Despite having been only a few months ago, I was in better shape then than now. I had someone to look forward to seeing at the end of the day, and she was always waiting. Elouise. The little gear head I knew growing up that had become my girlfriend after quite a strange turn of events. At first I had my eyes on Sena, and Jude on Elouise, but after we both got rejected and told the truth of who they liked, you could say it was inevitable one would go to the other. But the details of that story didn't hold too much relevance that led into homecoming night.

It was something Elouise wanted to do. Since I'd leave often, there was hardly enough time for the two of us to just be. So she begged me to have a day for ourselves, hence the Homecoming night dance. If only she'd known what deal I had made with Jackson prior.

They told me the words I'd dreaded and loathed: Elouise had to die. They gave me thirty days to make good on the plan, a plan that Elouise's parents agreed to. Thirty days to decide when and where Elouise died. And she'd given me the day. With two weeks to prepare, I was given all that time by Jackson to make good on my end, freeing me from typical duties. A nice dress for Elouise, a matching outfit for myself.

We shared a ride with Jude and Sena to the dance at our high school, held in its massive gymnasium with the theme "Night Over the Ocean".

It was the setup that led to her death. But in that single night, Elouise and I went even further in our relationship, sneaking off, doing as teenagers would in the spirit of love. I convinced myself I should give her one night of pleasure, one she'd always treasure. But in the heat of the moment, I almost forgot what I was being forced to do. The moment we returned to our home, I knew men were in position. But they weren't to kill her. No, they were retrieval for her body.

I was put up to it because of my personal connection to Elouise. I loved her. She was my everything, my reason for living. For when I gave up on everything else when I lost my family, she reminded me she'd always be by my side. Through anger, strife, happiness and bliss, she'd be with me through it all. She swore by it. And Jackson forced me to put an end to her life that I swore to protect.

I'd never forget that night. I couldn't. It was always the nightmares I kept seeing.

She walked in front of me, telling me how it may as well have been the best night she'd ever had. How much she loved me.

I stood behind her, silent and bracing myself for the inevitable. I didn't have a choice.

"Bullshit! You mean to tell me there's no other way?" I had yelled at Jackson back at the warehouse lab.

"It's either her or both of you, Gabriel," Jackson proclaimed.

Those words were damning. If I refused, he'd leave us out to hang and dry for the wolves. And so…

I reached for her, grabbed her and pulled her in close. I embraced her body with my left, and stabbed her with my right. I held her close, my mouth to her ear and uttered my last words to her as her boyfriend… As her betrayer.

"Elouise… I don't expect you to forgive me…"

Elouise Gaines died that night, in my arms and by the very tool she'd given me only to be used to kill her. I had cried out in unmatched despair, wailing into the night that could only respond with silence for having betrayed my reason for living, the love of my life. The very sun I looked forward to, was now snuffed out by the dark hand that forced its way into my heart.

But there wasn't time for grieving. Jackson's men were quick to enter our home and not only did they take her body, but the dragged me along back to the warehouse. And what I bore witness there was my second count of betrayal to Elouise.

I woke up once again in the middle of the night, hot sweat soaking my clothes. I wasn't screaming or yelling bloody murder, I was actually sobbing without making a single noise. I couldn't mistake the tears that had been flowing from my eyes for sweat. I knew better than that. I kept staring at the ceiling without cause. My breathing was hoarse and labored. Most of all though, I was thirsty. My mouth was dry as Death Valley itself.

I slowly rose up from my bedding in my room and made headed downstairs to the kitchen. Once I made it to the cupboard, I grabbed a simple glass and poured water into it from the refrigerator that had a neat little drinking water nozzle installed. Elouise wasted no expense, having only the best money could buy. Though that TV would definitely need to be replaced in the morning. Or the next day.

Once I had my glass, I took a seat at the kitchen table and started sipping away while reflecting again on my past. But out of the corner of my eye, in the darkness of the house, I made out Raven, sitting on the couch with her legs tucked close to her chest with her arms. I wasn't aware of her presence before, and I wasn't sure she was aware of mine.

Regardless, it was odd seeing Raven in such a position. It was the first time I'd ever seen her in such a state that looked like she was suffering. And damn it, I was curious.

"Raven?" I called to her in the darkness.

She shot her head up in surprise, which caught me by surprise. And yes, I was seeing with enhanced night vision with my right eye, so everything was clear as day.

"Gabriel? I didn't see you there. You surprised me..." Raven said sullen. I could see some tear streaks on her cheeks.

What reason did she have to be crying?

I got up from my chair, abandoning my glass and walked over to Raven, still curled up on the couch.

"Are you alright? Something happen, Raven?" I asked out of nowhere. Never have I ever expressed any sort of concern over Raven until now. I still felt out of place. Usually she was the one asking me about my state.

Raven heaved a heavy sigh, but she brought it upon herself to look me dead in the face, with a halfhearted smile and the once hopeful dark brown eyes had become so distraught... and confused?

"I just had the worst nightmare..." she said recomposing herself. "I saw you... And Elouise. Together, here at this house."

What the...?

"And... I saw you kill her... A blade right through the chest..."

Impossible...

"It felt too real... But, that's all it was, right? Just a dream," Raven said practically to herself. She must've been traumatized by watching something like that, but for her to have that dream?

I sat down next to her and offered my embrace to her, which she quickly took immediately by grasping me like I had before.

"Don't worry, Raven, it was just a dream, none of that was real," I said, trying to convince myself that it wasn't anything to be concerned about, no matter how disturbing it was.

"I know," Raven said as she rested her head into my chest. "I mean, Elouise died in a car accident, and there's no way you'd ever do something like that."

My stomach practically jumped into my mouth. This was... This must have been mere coincidence. I wanted to think that. There was no way. Alexander programmed Raven's memory to avoid things like this... I needed to think more on this... First things first, I needed Raven out of earshot.

I offered to take Raven back to her room to sleep, to which she graciously accepted. After leading her back to bed, I went back downstairs again and furiously began to catalog potential risks and variables concerning Raven's mental psyche... And the potential her nightmare was an omen. I needed concrete answers.

In my desperation, I called the one man who I hated most, just so I could reach the one man who could help me.

Through my arm's internal communication systems, I tried contacting Jackson. After several minutes of ringing, he finally answered, and I didn't waste any time with pleasantries.

"I need you to get me into contact with Alexander, now," I demanded.

"Good morning to you too, Gabe... It's a little early to be making calls, wouldn't you agree—"

"I don't care!" I said sharply, but quietly. Last thing I wanted was for my sin given life to be poking her head into this part of my life. "I need him. Now. I know you can contact him, Jackson. It's about her."

Jackson was silent for a moment, but I could hear through my earpiece that I used with my arm for phone calls like this that he was moving about from his position of rest.

"I can't make promises, Gabriel," Jackson said more awake and alert, realizing how dire my situation was. "Remember, he's a man that prefers not to be found. It's highly likely I won't be able to simply contact him like before. I'll try my best, though. In the meantime, you should rest. Holiday vacation is no excuse to be lacking sleep."

With that he ended our call and I returned my earpiece back into my arm. But it didn't take more than a minute for my arm to be receiving another call. That was too fast, even for someone like him. I quickly accessed the communicator earpiece and answered the call.

"Alexander...?" I said cautiously.

"The one and the same," the voice of a rather familiar grandfatherly figure replied. "Good morning, Mister Ern. I understand you've got quite the predicament on your hands."

He knew? How?

"Let's not discuss how I know of your situation. It's simple. I've Raven's status monitored for any sort of anomaly that could raise concerns. Such as a nightmare."

"But how would that even—"

"It triggered a special alarm that indicated potential for the true personality to resurface. Hence my call."

"How do I stop it?"

"You can't. Or rather, it's impossible for you."

Why?

"I know I've told you before about potential triggers for Raven, and to be careful if one should present itself. However, something like this cannot be helped." Alexander continued explaining as if he knew everything that was happening was to be expected. "Physical triggers, such as photographs or other documentation of her previous life are easy enough to avoid. However, there is the potential the part of her subconscious that remembers who she really is can influence her mental state. In that regard, the only thing you can do to suppress and limit the effects of those triggers is to simply convince her to dismiss them as mere figments of her imagination."

"So lie to her…"

"Gabriel," Alexander called me to attention, as if he was ready to give me an ultimatum. "I am neither for or against this method concerning your overall situation. So my only words of advice in regards to Raven are: should you feel to fully awaken her true identity, be careful. For you may regret your decisions."

The call ended and I stood there, paralyzed from his advisement. No… It felt like it was a cautious encouragement. It was true, he never sided with or against me. All he ever did was to help improve the capabilities of my arm... And dealing with the fallout with Elouise...

Back when I had killed Elouise, when they took me and her back to that warehouse, Alexander had been waiting in his workshop that was constructed for him through his specifications. That night, I learned what Alexander specialized with. He didn't create the chaos generator to be used with my arm by mere coincidence. It was meant to act as a core for something bigger than an arm.

Alexander had been lured by Jackson with the promise to finally have the opportunity to put the years of research and development to use. And Elouise's body had been the perfect subject. Someone who was targeted, potentially for a large part of her life. If she disappeared, there'd be no reason to be after her. The car accident was just an alibi with convincing props to go along with, fake body, blood and all. No one would know any better. No one would ever go after Elouise ever again.

And yet, she still lived, through the guise of another identity. Raven. My worst sin given life.

As I stood silently in the dark, lonesome living room I once shared with Elouise, I stared out into the night sky, hoping for some sign; a sweet release from my own tortured self, racked with endless guilt and regret.

It was that moment that gave me a response to my own dilemma. The only way to find an end for the suffering was to force it. The only way to atone, is to face my own mistakes and accept the punishment I deserve.

At the end of the day, no matter what happens to me... At least Elouise would still be safe...

Chapter 4
Past, Present and Future

Anxiety flooded into me as my wakeup call woke me the next morning. My mind was racing with all manner of thoughts, ideas. Ways things could progress from bad to worse. After all, I had consigned myself to Elouise's whims. I wasn't ready for it, I would never be, but I wasn't ready to continue letting this lie of a life that we had continue.

Forget the details of a typical morning routine after waking up. I wasted no time going downstairs where I found Raven already preparing breakfast for us. Whatever she was cooking held no bearing on what I already decided was the ultimate objective to complete.

"Good morning Gabriel!" Raven greeted me, having not turned away from what she was currently cooking in that black skillet she was predominantly focused on. No doubt her cybernetics helped her detect my presence, and it was obvious I was behind her since I was the only other person who lived in this house.

But dammit, watching her cook like this, it reminded me of Elouise. Before I turned special operative boy, she only knew the life of a gear head and tech magician. After I started leaving for long periods of time, she quickly learned all manner of basic skills, like cooking and simple house chores I would have otherwise done with her. Beyond that, she was more accustomed to ordering delivery.

I missed her so much...

"Breakfast will be ready soon, if you want, you can wait at the table!" Raven said breaking me out of my reminiscing.

However, I walked toward her and placed my arm on her shoulder.

"Raven... We need to talk," I said solemnly. "Turn off the stove and come with me, please."

Raven looked over her shoulder in shock, but humored my request. Once she had rendered the stove completely risk-free, I led her to the foyer of the house. It had a couch where I remember Elouise planting a kiss on my cheek once, just to tease me when I had my heart set on Sena, and near it had been a larger dining table and a cupboard filled with extravagantly designed porcelain plates. But it was beneath it, the cabinets below that held my key to freeing Elouise.

I left Raven standing by herself, allowing her to watch me as I knelt next to the cabinet doors. Before, I had told her to never reach into them. When I opened them, inside had been all manner of dangerous items that could've jogged her memory. The "triggers" had been a collection of pictures of Elouise before her death. One of which I had chosen almost immediately as my weapon of choice. It was a picture of me, Sena, Jude and Elouise, months before she had died. When the four of us had gone on a double date and had someone else on the streets take a picture of us in front of a mural.

"Raven," I called to her as I stood up with the photo in my hand. Once I saw I had her full undivided attention, without any question, I raised my hand to her, practically shoving the picture into her vision for her to see.

"Who do you see in this picture?" I demanded from her.

Raven had initially shown no sign of emotion at staring at the photo. But soon, she began wincing at the picture. I could tell confusion was running rampant on her internal memory.

"Who... Who is that?" She asked.

"You can't recognize her? This is Elouise, before she died," I told her outright.

"But she... She looks like me... The hair, eyes and skin tone may be different, but she looks like... me..."

Subtle changes, but enough to throw off even the best visual identification software, had been done on Elouise. Before, she'd been more fair-skinned, thanks to always being shut inside her own shop in the basement. In comparison, Raven was darker, her facial features had been meant to give a meaner, sharper expression. Just how I'd seen her in my nightmares.

Elouise had a much softer expression, kinder, bubbly even. That was how I chose to remember her, but because Raven had never really seen what Elouise looked like, she'd never known just how similar she really was. Everyone else was fooled, but I always knew. As for Raven, the artificial memories implanted in her made her believe a different version of Elouise was hers. Not the bonafide article.

Raven knew what she looked like, but presented with this, she was quick to tell Elouise was far too similar to her. It was plainly obvious from her warping expressions.

But… Why…? Why do I remember that day, too?" She asked, her voice quivering.

Sudden tears that had pooled around her eyes had astonished her as she wiped them away with a finger, but never ripping the sight of the photo from her view.

"You want to know why? It's because you, Raven, never really existed before now," I glared directly into her eyes without remorse. "In fact, you were someone else before."

I stepped toward her with the photo, like I was exorcising a ghost out of her body with a crucifix.

"Do you really know who you are?" I demanded.

"I'm… Raven… No, that's not correct?" Raven said questioning herself. She started to panic from the anxiety. "Elouise… She helped me, and made me promise that I would—"

"Stop. That memory is fake. Elouise never met you. You are just a fabricated personality. A replacement for the real person you were before."

Raven started backing away, afraid of the picture practically, but I kept closing the distance until she backed into a wall, cornering herself. I wanted her to face this.

"Why are you doing this?" Raven asked terrified. "I'm seeing visions of memories I don't have… Or did I have them? I don't know what's happening! Tell me, please! Why?"

"Remember who you are, you walking replacement part," I said angrily. "If you really want to know why, then remember."

Raven went wide-eyed, but then in an instant, they glazed over as she slumped to her knees and closed her eyes.

I lowered the photo to my side as I stared down at her. With my cybernetics, I was able to gather that Raven had undergone a complete reset of her systems, essentially shutting down even her consciousness. And she was rebooting quickly.

Her face began twitching as she was slowly regaining consciousness.

"Raven?" I called to her cautiously as I slowly knelt over in front of her.

When I didn't receive a response, I steeled myself with a deep breath and prepared for another attempt at reaching out to her.

"Elouise…?" I said quietly near her.

***

Everything was so empty at first, nothing but black and deafening silence. But slowly, noise became clearer. The silence was replaced with a familiar boy's voice, one that was run ragged and weary from months of self-sacrifice and self-destructive acts.

Gabriel. The man I loved… Now was nothing more to me than a damn traitor. Oh, I remembered everything. Even after being killed, I could see the memories of what they replaced me with. What he was forced to live with. I knew they were behind it all, but the fact of the matter was: they handed him the gun and he willingly squeezed the trigger on my life.

My eyes gradually split open from being shut, my HUD booting up and giving me updates on my systems as I rebooted. This pissed me off even more. I was a cyborg now. Me. The girl who wanted to change the world for the better with my cybernetic advancements, now made into a weapon of mass destruction. And for what? To satisfy the needs of the people Gabriel worked for?

"Elouise?" I heard him call to me again as I slowly looked up at him, blankly meeting his eager expression. I hoped he was anticipating something better, because I still remember his words from that night…

"I don't expect you to forgive me."

My face contorted into furious, indignant rage and I roared at him, tackling him onto his back. My cybernetics allowed me to easily overpower him as I slammed him hard and pinned him with my arms and legs on the carpet. I raised my left hand off his chest, and transformed it into a superheated blade, and rammed it into his shoulder.

Gabriel cried out in agony as he grasped onto my bladed arm with the one I gave him. The thing I believed he would have used to protect me until the day he died. I was baring my teeth at him like a rabid animal, my own seething fury emanating all over him like the sun. Unyielding and punishing.

"You traitor!" I screamed at him beneath me. "I trusted you! I believed in you! I gave you everything! I loved you! And this is how you pay me back?"

"Agh! Elouise!" Gabriel called to me, trying to get in his own words.

"I remember everything, Gabe!" I continued in my tirade. "Everything!"

I shoved the blade deeper into his shoulder, eliciting more pain from him. But it wasn't enough. I wanted him to experience the pain of the man he had in a similar position from way back then. From the night he and I finally became a couple and were attacked by my parent's rivals. He protected me then. So what the hell changed now?

"So why? Why did I have to die, Gabe? Why?"

"I didn't have a choice!" Gabe said almost immediately.

"Liar! You've always had a choice!"

"No! I didn't! They may have put me up to it, but even your parents promoted it! They approved of it all!"

What...

"Loaded horseshit!" I shouted in anger.

"I'm not lying, I swear!" Gabriel protested. Suddenly his grip loosened and let his arm drop away, just as his entire body seemed to go limp. He was resigning. "But that doesn't matter... I killed you... There's no denying that. I stole everything from you and let them turn you into this, just because they said it'd save you..."

I could see tears welling up in his eyes.

"I never wanted this; I just wanted to protect you. But I let them control me, and became trapped by their whims... I couldn't let things continue as they were... That's why I chose to make you remember... To put it all to rest!"

He wanted to die...

"So go ahead, kill me. It won't make things worse off than they already are. Jackson and his group will leave you alone, just as those bastards that have been targeting you will. This is what I deserve!"

Watching Gabriel become so pathetic, so broken had pacified my anger at him. He used to be so strong, despite what the life he had now was doing to him. I remember why he continued going strong, because he told me at the end of it all, I was always waiting for him at home, ready to receive him. I was his everything.

Now he was wanting nothing but the end of it all, with his life no less. We were only fifteen… We shouldn't have been subjected to this farce we called a life. When I look at what he and I had become, it was sobering, to the point I could only pity Gabriel for what he had devolved into.

I pull the blade out from Gabriel, making him cry out in pain once more as I stood over him.

"I won't kill you, Gabe… You don't deserve to die like this…" I told him outright staring down at him, becoming his judge, jury and executioner. "You're wrong to think I won't forgive you either… But with the way things are, it isn't going to be immediate… I will always remember this, and I want you to as well, because I believe you are not beyond redemption, Gabe…"

I walked over him and headed to the sliding door in the kitchen area of our house. It was still daytime, but the clouds had been rather heavy for today. How cliched was that? It was so dumb, so cheesy that something like this had to have happened on a cloudy day. What'd make it even more laudable would be if it had been pouring like the end of the world was near.

I opened the sliding door and stepped out into the backyard, feeling the stone patio underneath my bare feet. It was strange to be feeling from that part of my body. Cybernetic limbs I may have, but they felt too organic. Whatever they did to me was more advanced than anything I've ever produced-No, this was that old man Alexander's work, he was the brains behind it all. And I was probably decades behind him. As I stepped out onto the verdant green grass and stared up into the sky, I grew agitated…

So much on my mind, all the things that had happened to me and Gabe… I hated it.

I hated what they forced him to do.

I hated how they treated him like a tool.

I hated them for having made me into something I've only ever dreamed of, but never could reach.

I hate it. I hate it. I hate it. I hate it!

"AAAAAAAAAAAAAUUUUUUUUUGH!"

My anguished cry out to the sky was my way of cursing my very being, to whoever anyone called their higher power. I gripped my hair, only to lash my arms out, fully transforming them into automatic sub-machine guns and peppered the walls surrounding the yard in a quick barrage. I collapsed to my knees and began wailing profusely with my arms hung next to my legs.

My cybernetics detected Gabe approaching from behind, but I was no longer feeling any sort of maliciousness toward him. I looked over my shoulder and saw his head hung low, his shoulder being held with his human arm like it would fall off if it didn't.

We were silent with each other at this point, but we instinctively knew that we didn't want to be alone. He sat down next to me with his good side and I found myself leaning into his body almost on reaction. I used his shirt at a means to keep wiping away the tears that streamed from my eyes as we stayed there throughout the day. Silently.

Day gradually became sunset as the clouds cleared and the setting sun graced the sky. I didn't feel the slightest bit hungry and I guess neither did Gabe. He eventually laid his head over mind, finding some comfort in the fact I was willing to let him.

"Gabe," I called to him quietly. "I know you've been having nightmares about that night... And before you even speak, I want you to know, while I'm willing to forgive you, you have to come to terms with yourself as well, otherwise you'll be endlessly tortured by it. Don't even try to argue, because I've seen enough through Raven's eyes."

Gabe remained silent, but he understood. His head slightly pressed into mine in response.

"For now, we should go back inside... Figure out what to do next..."

As I slowly stood, Gabe looked up with such a lost expression, it made him look more like an abandoned child... Kind of how he was when he lost his parents.

"Like what?" He asked weakly.

"First and foremost, I think I owe my parents a well-deserved phone call..."

Chapter 5
No More Secrets

After helping Gabe patch up the wound I had left in his shoulder, I led him back into the house and toward the hallway that led to the garage from the living room. But in that hallway was a massive metal door that led to the basement. That basement was converted, by me, into my personal machine shop. It was where I kept all of my mechanical innovations and where I worked… used to work on them.

It was also where I operated on him to give him his new arm and other cybernetic implant. At this point in time, after remembering and waking up to wanting to kill him outright, I felt maybe I was the one responsible for all of his despair. When I trace it all back, I took him into my home, I gave him the arm, I'm the one who became his girlfriend because I told Jude I loved Gabe more. If it wasn't for me, Gabe, would have never been involved in my life as much as he was now. He wouldn't have had been forced to become the fractured man he was now.

But I couldn't dwell on it. I refused to. Most others would look to the past and reflect on it heavily. I don't. I've never looked back on many of the things I've done. I've always looked forward to what lay ahead. It's funny when I do think about myself like that. I remember how Gabe used to tease me about history class I had to take back in eighth grade and how much I've hated it. I never like it.

But like I said: always forward, never looking back. Especially now, since of all the people I could blame for this mess of a life I now had as an unwilling cyborg patsy for myself, there were two in particular I could confront directly, or as directly one could through a video call.

That's right, I was making a video call, to a certain couple of business tycoons, that served as my own mother and father. Soon to be demoted and subsequently removed in every aspect of my life.

My workshop had been massive, easily spanning the entire property area, to which is saying: its freaking big. Right in the center of it all was a tower of technology I called my programming station, also used for casual usage whenever I feel the need for a much needed respite. And hanging over the super desktop computer were four large display screens, all of which face four different directions. I had set them up so where ever I was in the workshop, I'd be able to maintain a video call and whoever it was on the other line would be able to view me as I worked on my machines. At least that was how it used to be before my and Gabe's life became a twisted mess.

So, imagine the surprise my parents displayed at the sight of me, with Gabe practically keeping to the rear as if hiding in the shadows. At first, they looked anxious to see if it was me as Elouise calling them, but looked confused when all they saw was the replacement Gabe was forced to be with.

"Surprise, mom, dad," I said halfheartedly, calling them out on their existence in my life. "It's your daughter, in the flesh, so to speak…"

They stared speechless. Of course. How could they properly respond? They pretty much consigned me to death. Just looking at me now, and hearing the way I talk and what I am going to tell them outright was going to do more than destroy their psyches.

"Well, if you won't talk, then I'll tell you everything I want to you both," I continued with vicious edge to my voice. "You two, are despicable. You don't deserve to be called parents. Let alone have the privilege to procreate."

My parents' eyes widened when they heard those words come out of my mouth. I had fired at them with such animosity, but it was merely a taste. After I'm done with these clods, even Mother Teresa wouldn't help them.

"I want you to look at me, and I dare you to say you didn't let those assholes that you had protect us, force Gabe to murder me!" I turn and point at Gabe, practically putting him in the spotlight as he turned his head away in shame. "Look at him! Look at what you two have done to him! He's been put through a hell no kid should ever have experienced. But he did it anyway because he genuinely loved me! He's been here more than you two have ever been!"

I never once looked back at Gabe, only because I wanted my parents to see my unbridled fury for what it was. I wanted them to understand I absolutely hated them. That of all the people I've ever had the displeasure of knowing, they were the worst kind of existence to me. The level equitable to that of slime.

"I was willing to endure through it all, too! The days he'd be gone, all the pain we'd go through, we'd be able to handle it all together! And now, he's barely holding himself together! Suffering from nightmares from what he's done, he's barely holding on at this point!"

I fully faced them, having made my point clear with Gabe's present state. This wasn't just for me, this was for him. I wanted him to realize I do not put blame solely on him, that I was being honest when I said I was willing to forgive him.

"So, if nothing else, here's my final proclamation. My ultimatum: I do not ever, ever want to see, or hear from either of you ever again. You two aren't my parents anymore," I snapped my arms up at the displays, transforming them into arm guns. "You're just people that conceived me. Nothing more. Goodbye."

I fired both firearms, having used the firepower to completely destroy the displays. All manner of electrical sparks and broken metal peppered the floor around the area. A fitting end to my final call to those two. I turned about, having reformed my arms back into their default settings. Gabe had stared at me with such a hollow and pitiful look, but considering what just happened… I couldn't blame him. So I tried my best to give him an endearing smile, as if to say things were going to be okay. But my chest felt heavy. It couldn't have been from what I just did, no way. Screw those people. They put us through this.

But… They only tried to protect me… They… They always did what they could for me, they'd call me when they could, even when Gabe wasn't around. They wanted to let me know they loved me, even from the world over.

Always apologizing for missing my birthday, but making it up for it by making a call together and sing happy birthday to me with a cake on both ends.

I can remember why they did it, not just from what Gabe told me, but from the fact I had a memory of it that he wasn't aware of. Even though I blamed them for it… I can still…

"Hey, that went well, didn't it?" I asked Gabe as he continued to stare at me.

His hollow expression seemed to gain life as he seemed surprised at me. I could feel something strange slowly dripping down my cheeks.

"Elouise… You're…" He muttered.

"Huh?" I wiped my face with my hands, finding that actual human tears had been streaming from my eyes. "Hey this isn't funny… I'm not even human anymore, right? I'm more machine than organic? So… Why? Why am I crying over them?"

Gabe rushed to me and embraced me tightly. Even with his recovering injury, he still had the strength for this. The strength I had before seemed to fade away, and I was slowly reduced to a sobbing mess once more. Gabe's shoulder was the only thing to find comfort in now. His body was now the closest thing I had to find some sort of warmth. I grabbed onto him, desperate to feel like I still had life in me, that I still had a chance in this world.

"What do we do now?" I asked him, now lost in my way having just disowned my own family.

"It's like you said, Elouise," Gabe said gently. "We continue to figure out our lives… Where we go from this next? We can't keep Jude and Sena in the dark about this anymore. We need to tell them, too."

When the both of us went to bed that night, we slept separately. Elouise needed more time to adjust to her life now that she was a reborn cyborg with the memories she had as Raven. As for me, I was fine with sleeping alone again. However, when I woke up in the middle of the night, I found myself with Elouise next to me on the floor of my room, but she was wide awake. She told me she didn't need to sleep, at the same time, she didn't want to be alone, so she snuck into my room and lay near me for comfort. So for the first time in months, I slept with the girl I loved right next to me.

The days were too damn slow leading up to the morning of our return to school came. Before then, it had been so awkward between us that I had no idea to really break the tension. He'll you could cut a knife through it all.

On the morning of back to school, Elouise had gotten up before me and had breakfast made and woke me up so we could eat together. And I was glad to have done so. For the first time, I woke up without any sort of animosity, no aggression. For the moment, it was bliss being able to eat with Elouise as she met me with the gentle warm smile I've remembered and longed for so long. But soon, we got ready for what the day really had in store for us.

We met Jude and Sena at the bus stop as normal, but even they picked up something was off about us. Elouise kept silent, keeping up the Raven persona for the time being. I told both of them we needed to talk about something heavily important, but only once we made it to school and in private.

It was at the track and field of our school that I told them my part of the story, and then Elouise, telling them who she really was all along, told them hers. Their faces spoke volumes on how much they were overwhelmed by the truth they had been presented with. In fact, they were speechless.

Elouise and I had been standing before them, silent, waiting for them to say anything. After all we said, all we could really do was wait for a response.

"Wow..." Jude said placing his hand over his short-cut brown hair, scratching his head in amazement. "That's... a lot to take in, man..."

I took that as a good sign from Jude, having spoken first. While he said it without too much negative or positive bias, it was still reassuring he wanted to comprehend the information given.

"But, I guess I get it," he continued.

I breathed a sigh of relief as Sena seemed to even smile at Jude's declaration.

"Ah, well, I'm glad you understa—"

A massive wallop from Jude's fist shut me up and laid me out on the turf. I was sprawled out, still trying to comprehend that my friend just sucker punched me.

"Jude?" Sena cried out.

I remained stunned on the floor, staring up at Jude, but slowly becoming agitated that he seemingly lied.

"I understand you're a goddamn coward," Jude said angrily.

Seeing him over me with clenched fists and a furious expression, it was still a shock. He never looked at me like that, with so much disdain like I'd just snuck around behind his back and did unspeakable things to Sena.

"You loved her, right? You said you wanted to protect her no matter what, right?" Jude threw at me, using my words against me. "So how come you didn't try and protect her like you said? Why kill her and turn her into this? If I was in your shoes, I would have at least made an attempt!"

He came in closer to punch me again, but hearing those words out of his mouth had pissed me off. *He thinks he could've done better than me?* Before he could even land his punch, my right arm, with its superior functionality, mechanical advantage and speed, quickly caught his fist, holding it with ease. It allowed me, in my now enraged state of mind, to get up and ram my left knuckles into Jude's jawline, knocking him back, but not onto the floor.

"You think you can do better than me? You think you could've done what I have?" I shouted at Jude appalled at his arrogance. "Fuck you! You'd die without having done shit!"

Jude let those words sink in before he lunged at me, trying to tackle me to the ground. Instead of letting him have his way, I wrapped my arm around his neck and fell with him, letting his head hit the floor as I locked my choke on him.

"So why didn't you try?" Jude said, straining to get free. "I would have given it a shot, I would have—"

"You would've died in vain!" I yelled at him.

"Guys stop!" Sena begged us. But we both were suffering from tunnel vision. We were the only two people that mattered at the moment.

Jude managed to lift my entire body up while I had him in the hold and slammed me into the floor, causing me to lose my grip from getting the wind knocked out of me. But I recovered quick enough to kick him off. We both got back up on our feet and started wailing on each other, but we were no kids playing slap fight. He was a well-built football player now, and I was a killing machine with military training to match special forces.

"You're a worthless scumbag, Gabe!"

"You're nothing more than an arrogant son of a bitch!"

"Stop, please!"

We were deep into our fisticuffs, no longer willing to listen to any outside force, no matter who or where it came from. Jude may have pined for Elouise at one point, but I was her boyfriend. I was the one who willingly took the burden of protecting her.

"Guys… This is enough," Elouise called out. "Stop making Sena cry alre—"

She got cut off, but I didn't know by what. It could've been by me, or Jude, but she didn't make a noise when someone may have missed their mark with their punches. It didn't matter to us. We wanted to tear each other apart just to make a point.

We just wanted to—

"AAAAAAAAUGH!"

"GAAAAAAAAH!"

A familiar but intense paralyzing pain coursed throughout my body, making my every muscle contract forcibly beyond normal human capacity. The was the effect I knew ever so fondly that'd been associated with a taser.

I was on the ground along with Jude, just a few inches away, paralyzed and in pain, but I could see the cables that were delivering the voltage that rendered us immobile.

Though, for some reason, this was beyond normal levels acceptable even by law enforcement.

"I said to quit it!" Elouise's voice rang out angrily.

The taser cables that attached to my body quit surging electricity through my body and I was able to barely move my head to see Elouise who looked like someone had punched her cleanly across the face. And she was beyond irate.

Oh great, now we had pissed her off.

"Elouise?" I said, strained, trying to recover from the electrical shock.

Jude and I slowly sat upright as Elouise walked closer to us, but ready to jolt us even more should we show any sign of aggression. Though we were pretty much incapable of moving very much as I looked to Jude who wore a similar worried expression I had whenever Elouise was angry. It wasn't the first time she was like this, but she didn't have access to cybernetics like this before.

"First of all, shame on you two for acting like brats!" Elouise shouted. "Jude, Gabe and I wanted to confide in you and Sena because of how things were. The only reason we didn't before is because we didn't want to risk you two being targeted like us! But things have changed, like we have explained! So for you, Jude, to call him out like this? Absolutely abhorrent. You two are like brothers, aren't you?"

"But—"

"No! I don't care what you think you could've done!" Elouise cut Jude off before he could defend himself. "Fact of the matter is, Gabe was the one on the spot, not you. You could preach about whatever you want, but it wouldn't change a damn thing! And Gabe!"

Oh great.

"Shame on you for engaging Jude like this! I expected better! The most I'd expect is for you to simply defend, never strike back! Friends shouldn't be trying to kill each other like this!"

"To be fair, Elouise... Friends don't taser friends either," I decided to say. Which may have been a damning sentence for me.

Elouise narrowed her eyes at us, regarding us like the brats she had referred to us as.

"At the rate you two were going at it? If not a taser, would you have rather me used non-lethal ammunition to make you submit?"

"Not exactly what he was going for, Elouise—"

"You shut up! Especially since you punched me in the face... Jerkwad..." Elouise said with disdain.

Oh man, there went some points for Jude...

Jude shut his mouth up instantly and I couldn't help but chuckle.

He stared back at me pathetically as if to say "It's like she never really died..."

I gave him a smirk and shrugged. Like my response was, "Well, technically, you wouldn't be wrong..."

"Hey, quit that! I can tell you two are talking like I'm not here!" Elouise pouted.

I laughed a bit as did Jude. Sena who was behind Elouise seemed to loosen up as well as she walked up to her and placed a hand on her shoulder with a giggling smile.

"Hey... Sorry about earlier man," Jude said apologetically. "I just got heated up when you told me how she really died. I shouldn't have called you out like that."

"I'm sorry too, bro," I quickly said. "I mean, I got pretty pissed off, and was about ready to kill you."

"Guess we were really just dumbasses trying to prove a stupid point, huh?"

"Hey, no reason we shouldn't move on, right?"

I reached out to Jude with my hand and he grasped it with his, gripping it firmly. We both smiled like idiots having just recently been trying to beat the crap out the other.

"Ahem! Are you forgetting something, dummies?" Elouise interrupted our bro moment and we soon saw she was still annoyed with us.

"Oh, right, ah ha, sorry about, y'know, hitting you Elouise," Jude said panicked. "Heat of the moment, right Gabe?"

"Whoa, dude, don't try to drag me under the bus with you," I said trying to cover myself. "If you're going into another fight I'm staying out of it. I've already seen enough of Elouise pissed off, and I'm really don't want to die now. Should've seen how she dealt with her parents."

"That bad huh?"

"Ugh... Boys..." Elouise groaned in defeat. I felt the cables detach from my body with a wince of pain as Elouise reverted her arms to normal.

Despite shaking her head at us, she was smiling, as if pleased with the outcome. Sena kept smiling away, confident in Elouise's ability to "defuse" the situation.

"No more fighting, alright?" Elouise asked.

Both of us smiled like idiots and agreed together.

"Now, about having been tasered…" Jude began slowly realizing the pain he was still in, "Am I going to be okay to do athletics today?"

The rest of conversation divulged into more teenage antics as Elouise mocked Jude for having been tasered a major issue. While Elouise assured Jude he'd be okay, I couldn't help but make note of how sore his muscles would be after the fact, leading into laughter by Sena. Eventually, the five minute warning bells rang, alerting us to the imminent routine of boring classes. I wanted nothing more than to skip as did Jude, but Elouise, activating her motherly mode, chastised us for it. Especially me. Telling me despite I had a free pass through high school, it still wasn't an excuse to do whatever I wanted. We all still laughed and started heading off to our classes like good students.

"Hey, Gabe," Jude called to me as we all walked together. "If you ever have free time or if you'd like, call on me-us, to hang out."

"Yeah, we've got your back no matter what, you two!" Sena said proudly with Jude.

Elouise and I both looked at them with cheerful smiles, glad that despite everything, those two were still our best friends we had.

"Thanks, you two!" Elouise and I said at the same time, ready for whatever lay ahead of us now.

Chapter 6
How Life Should Work...?

Elouise carried me on her shoulder back into our home. I was beaten, battered, and currently losing a large percentage of my own blood. We'd still been in our respective combat outfits, returning from another job. How I ended up in such a sorry state was easily explainable, but it definitely was anything but a funny story.

Jackson was quick to learn about Elouise's memories returning to her, but didn't care too much so much as her cover was kept intact. What that really meant was: the show must go on. So, it was about a week later when Elouise and I went on our first job together. The job this time: conduct an assault on a particular group's warehouses within the midwestern United States and reduce everything to mere refuse for landfills.

Simple enough, Elouise and I packed enough firepower between her body and my arm to take on whoever tried to stop us. But during the firefight we had, I got reckless, and charged headlong at the enemy. Using a powerful electromagnetic device in my arm, I was able to easily stop any bullets from hitting me, even from close range. When I got close however, I almost got overpowered and my leg was deeply cut by a combat knife.

Thanks to the nature of our mission, I couldn't afford to be slowed down, so I temporarily halted the bleeding with my right arm, creating a makeshift wrapping with nano machine-built cables. The rest of the mission was completed without too much else happening besides the wound. Even at the debriefing with Jackson, I was keeping it all together as the adrenaline rush I had worn off and the pain was setting in.

Elouise, of course, knew immediately the state I was in and was not amused about my stubborn method of ignoring my obvious wound. It was on the return trip home, transport provided by Jackson's people, that I was unable to hide it any longer. Elouise was forced to carry me out the vehicle to our home, but didn't have to provide some sort of excuse to our escort as he was simply tasked with just driving us, nothing more, nothing less. So caring of him.

Inside our home, Elouise placed me onto the couch in our foyer carefully. When she ripped apart my left pant leg to reveal the wound, I was sure the upholstery would get ruined from the eventual blood that would seep from the large gash in my leg. When Elouise saw how I had "treated" my wound, she grew visibly irritated at me, letting out an agitated groan of disgust.

"Dammit, Gabe," Elouise said under breath as she started going to work, removing the makeshift bandage. "How long were you planning on sleeping on this?"

"It's not as bad as it seems—"

"Don't give me that load of crap, Gabe!"

It may have been the blood loss I had already experienced, but I was so taken aback by Elouise's retort that I shut up. Despite how angry she seemed, her eyes told me she was more worried about the underlying reason behind my recent gaffe in the field.

"I'm not angry about you trying to hide this," she said as she began to work on stitching my wound closed with cyber cables from her more advanced repertoire of cybernetics. "But I am upset that you think it's okay for you to get injured this badly."

"It's nothing, Elouise," I tried to convince her otherwise, but once look at her pouting face said "hell no," but I was dead set on my stance. "Better me than you, either way."

That was met with a quick slap across the face from Elouise.

"Don't. Ever. Think. Or say anything like that again!" Elouise yelled at me while grabbing my hand. "I've told you before that I will forgive you for what you've done! But just because you can't find yourself able to, doesn't mean you can let yourself get hurt like this because you feel like you deserve it!"

I squeezed her hand while stifling my own emotions at hearing Elouise call me out for exactly the reason why I'd been in such a sorry state. I remember what she's said to me, I know she loves me enough to accept what I've done as a sick cruel twist of fate I couldn't escape. But that didn't mean I deserved even that much.

"Easy for you to say…" I said pathetically. "You aren't the one who held the trigger…"

"Does it look like I care about that? I care about you! I care enough to see you are hurting! You need to come to terms with what you've done. Yeah, easy enough for me to say, you're right, but no one said life was easy!"

I turn away from Elouise, finding it increasingly difficult to face her. I felt like I wanted to cry out of nowhere, because of how devoted she was to me, reminding me how much we depended on each other. Or rather, how dependent we have become on each other's being.

"Gabe?" Elouise called to me as I tried to hide from her. When I turned to face her, she was close to tears as well. Why the hell was I making her cry over me like this?

"Why are you crying?"

"I'm not crying, you're crying."

"Real mature, Elouise," I said half-jokingly. "Here I thought you were being the grown-up one."

"Shut up! I just want you to promise me you'll never get hurt like this again!"

Elouise tightened the grip on my hand again, staring into my eyes with hers, silently begging me to always stay with her.

"I can't promise I won't get hurt all the time, but, I can promise I won't be as reckless," I said outright. It was the most I could do in that regard after all. "And... I'm sorry... I didn't want you to cry..."

"You're damn right to be sorry, you ass," Elouise said with a smile while wiping away some of her tears. "Now wait here, you've lost a lot of blood, I'm going to go grab some for you."

Just as Elouise let go, I was surprised and confused as to where she was getting blood from. I was still a little light-headed from the blood loss I had, so when I tried sitting up I ended up laying back down, unable to catch Elouise as she made her way toward the living room. So I connected through our link to send her my question behind the blood.

Where I'm getting the blood? Why, from my workshop, of course! Or did you already forget how I attached that arm to you the first time?

Oh yeah, how could I forget. Elouise may have been a genius, and a licensed surgeon at the age of freaking fifteen, but she was only one person with a few helping arm drones. When she was operating on me to attach my arm, I hemorrhaged a lot of blood. Thankfully, she put me under the entire time, but she told me how she was almost scared she was going to lose me. But her being her, she was quick to rebound and successfully implant my cybernetics and even have a personal victory parade. It was just like her.

When Elouise returned with several pints of blood bags and catheter to put the blood into my body, I couldn't help but notice the cheerful smile Elouise wore, somehow finding all of this to her enjoyment.

"I swear it was like five minute ago you were upset at me," I remarked mischievously. "With that smile, you could've fooled me to believe otherwise."

"And here I thought you were both wallowing in your own pity and blood loss," Elouise shot back giving a wry smile. "But seeing how you're able to make jokes like that, you could've easily fooled me."

I chuckled, finding our banter reassuring that things could be worse. And I found more comfort feeling that our relationship, despite the terrible hand we've been played, won't fall apart that easily.

"What're you smiling so much about?" Elouise asked as she found the right spot to insert the needle for the blood bag on my left arm. "Y'know, you could've been hurt a lot worse had the guy angled his knife just right. Your femoral artery was a hair's breadth away from being nicked."

"Good to know, but it's just..." I trailed off, garnering Elouise's curiosity as she finished setting up the blood bag and was now keeping the blood flowing with her arm raised overhead. "It might be the blood loss speaking but, you're too good for me Elouise. You really are."

She blushes at that declaration, but still kept smiling. Knowing her, she'd be thinking "damn right I am!" However when she gave a small childish laugh, it kind of caught me off guard.

"Funny, I used to think you were the exact same thing for so long," Elouise said aloud.

Well, that... I had nothing for. Of all the things for her to tell me without hesitation, that single declaration left me stumped. I was too good for her at a point in time? When the hell was this and why...? Wait a second. If memory still serves me right, even having lost a lot of blood, Elouise had liked me since we were pipsqueaks... Then does that mean...

"I like how you're puzzling it all together in your right in front of me, Gabe," Elouise said teasingly, snapping me out of my train of thought.

Giving a proper response was still a damn near impossible task for my brain to handle at the moment due to the girl I loved revealed she used to have that kind of mentality when it came to romance. Geeze, I'm not one to talk, look where I'm at now!

"You clearly need time to dwell on that a bit, it's easy to tell," Elouise playfully said to break the silence. "Get some rest for now, I'll find something for the blood bag to hang from while you rest."

Elouise reached over and planted a quick smooch to my cheek, leaving my dumbfounded ass slightly flush from the sudden display of affection. Though I didn't mind it one bit, haha.

Elouise left me on the couch while she walked off to find a suitable object for the aforementioned blood, but before she could get too far…

"Hey, Elouise," I called, making her turn around to meet me. "I know this isn't exactly the best of times, but I enjoyed talking like that again. Between the two of us I mean."

Elouise gave a heart-melting smile at me, letting her eyes widen in joy as she cutely held her hands behind her back.

"There'll be more times like that Gabe," she told me in her old upbeat, spirited tone. "And we'll love those moments too as well! Get some rest now, okay? You deserve that much."

I nodded and laid back into the couch. It didn't take long for me to quickly doze off into a deep sleep. I wasn't worried about it in the slightest. My cybernetic HUD told me I would be just fine…

As quickly as I fell asleep, I woke up to the familiar smell and sound of olive oil frying some beef in our kitchen. Figured Elouise must've been cooking dinner. So I decided to remove the catheter in my arm, using my arm to stem the bleeding from the site.

I walked into the kitchen, taking in all the aroma from Elouise's cooking, something I'd always find nostalgic from the times before when she forced herself to learn when I wasn't around as much. I snuck up behind her, placing my hands squarely on her hips as I pressed closer gently on her back. Just hanging slightly on her shoulder, going ear to ear.

"Hey, babe, what're you cooking up tonight—" I choked up once I took a look at what she was really cooking.

In the skillet pan in front of her was a human heart that had all manner of blood and juices coming out from it. The worst part was that it was still beating.

I slowly backed away in horror, trying to keep from upchucking anything I still had in my guts from today. But when Elouise turned to face me, I dry heaved, hard enough to possibly dislodge my lungs. Before my very eyes, Elouise's entire front was blood-soaked from her chest down to her thighs. Right where her heart would have been, a gaping hole was just leaking blood all over her.

"What's the matter, Gabe?" She asked in such a deadpan manner that it reminded me more of how she was as Raven. "You did take my heart and rip it out. I figured you'd love it even more if you just ate it as well."

She began to smile with such a deranged twist of her head, even her eyes widened with insanity glowing through them, boring into my soul.

She stepped forward, trying to approach me. I was quick to wheel about and start to run, but instead ran into Elouise again, this time however, she held a knife in her hand, trembling with furious rage that blazed in those eyes of hers. She looked like how she was the night I killed her, blood stains and all.

"You should've never let me remember everything," she said through gritted teeth. "I was better off dead!"

Elouise raised the knife, flipping it overhead, aiming it at me and drove it down at full force. All I did was stare in confoundment; I'd been paralyzed by fear and struck with resignation to my fate that I stared at the knife as it drew closer in painstakingly slow motion.

This is how I'm meant to die...

"No!" I shouted at the last second, reaching out in defiance of my own self-prescribed comeuppance.

Everything went dark, but my eyelids shot open from the fresh hell I'd been subjected to. I met the real world panting in fear and shot upright, trying to defend from the knife in my dream. I was sweating bullets from just about every single pore of my body that wasn't machine as I frantically searched around, desperate to defend myself from some unknown force.

"Gabe! I'm here! It's okay! It was just a nightmare, a dream!" I heard Elouise shout at me, slowly jostling my cognitive senses back to normal. It was at this point I had recognized that she was holding me tightly, trying to keep me from losing my life.

I couldn't speak, or make much of an effort to communicate in any form. My mind had undergone such trauma the only way I could express my current state of mind was to grab hold of Elouise and start crying hoarsely into her shoulder.

"Cry as much as you want, Gabe," she said to me endearingly into my ear. "I'm here for you. Always. Just, don't give up on yourself. Keep trying. Please."

After a moment, I could feel Elouise begin to sob as well.

A pitiful, broken mess of a man. That was what I was now. But Elouise was hell-bent on making sure I'd somehow get pieced together. Made whole and not like Humpty Dumpty, but complete and better. She was hoping for too much, but I didn't want to let her down now, especially since that moment from earlier made me believe so much now more than ever.

Chapter 7
Twist

I woke up in the middle of the night in a cold sweat, panic setting in like I was trapped in a cage all of a sudden. But really, I was in the same bed as Elouise would have been.

Several weeks passed, several more missions, several minor injuries endured, but nothing prepared me for what began the day before. Jackson had a special assignment in mind for Elouise and only her alone. Which left me confused why I was being left out. After all, my contract for his protection was between me and him. Not Elouise. Then he slapped me across the face verbally by stating that Elouise was dead and as far as we were concerned, Raven acted as an extension of my own person, therefore, he was free to use her by herself in whatever matter he saw fit.

Elouise told me everything would be just fine after she received her orders. But I told her how much I didn't want her to go, if anyone was to run lone wolf, it should have been me. And before I was collected to be returned home, she gave me a quick kiss and told me, "at least you'll be safe."

I would be safe? What about you, you freaking idiot? That should be me out there. Me. I'm the one to be sent out into the frying pan. Not her. She shouldn't have to be a part of the mess I volunteered to be in.

I look up the time and found it was only four in the morning, still too damn early for a Saturday... Maybe not too early to make a call though.

I dialed in Jude's number, messaging him if he would be free today, hoping he would see it. With the message delivered, I laid back into my bed, expecting an answer in a few hours. To my shock, he responded within minutes.

Hey man, everything alright with you?

Just having a rough time sleeping, you're up kind of early, aren't you?

Yeah, but saw it was you so I woke myself up. And "trouble sleeping", huh? Something to do with Elouise being gone still, huh?

Read like a damn book. It went without saying Jude knew Elouise had been gone. So it was inevitable I'd find myself wanting to rely on him to help me cope with the absence of Elouise. Though I'd hoped I wasn't being too invasive...

Yeah. It's rough on me. Shocker, right? I was hoping we could hang out like we used to back then? Unless you have other plans of course.

Hey man, I said if you'd need anything that I'd be here. Sena, too. And yeah we were going to hang out today, but hey, there's always room for you bro.

Thanks man. Sorry if I cramp your style.

Lol, don't worry about it. If anything you'd help me out by keeping the undesirables away from Sena.

Funny... If anything does happen, I'll keep her safe. You're on your own at that point!

I'll tell Elouise.

Oh god no, why? That's like worse than death!

See you around ten then?

Sounds like a date. I'll be sure not to tell Sena you're secretly cheating on her.

Haha, glad to see you're doing better, bro. See you soon.

I chuckled to myself after that exchange between us. It actually helped my psyche recover greatly. Enough to the point I was able I lay back into the bed and relax without succumbing to some variation of anxiety.

I've got a good feeling about today.

However, I ended up falling asleep and only woke up when Jude messaged me about an hour and a half before ten. He told me he'd be picking me up with Sena and to have some swimwear ready as we were heading to the beach.

Dude. It's still winter and you want to head to the beach?

Didn't realize you didn't want to hang out. Don't tell me ol' badass Gabe is afraid of a little winter beach weather?

Eat me. I'll be ready for you guys when you get here. Your dad driving us?

Yeaup. Still no license, so gotta deal with it. He won't stick around though. He'll leave us alone once we're at the beach.

Alright. See you guys soon.

I preemptively checked the weather outlook for today and found it to be clear and sunny with temperatures averaging a high of about seventy. How lucky…

Even less lucky: I just realized the implications of going to the beach with how I looked physically. In the time I had been doing missions for Jackson, I only ever once found myself wearing nothing but shorts in the surf when I had been undergoing my training. So one: I've never been anywhere this public before and two: the only real swim trunks I had were my old, black training shorts.

Back when I wasn't so well developed, I was scrawny, even my cyber arm reflected that with having been smaller than it was currently. And now, I was feeling self-conscious about my appearance. Last thing I wanted was drawing undesired attention. Such that could spoil over Jude's and Sena's day. *Screw it, I'll manage. After all, what no one sees won't hurt them!*

At least that was the idea…

The beach was, to my dismay, pretty active with people taking advantage of the sun and fun to be had. Leave it to me to decide today was the best day to hang out with Jude and Sena…

After Jude's dad left us with all our stuff to include blankets, beach umbrella and various other beach necessities, Jude and Sena wasted no time in jumping into the surf, practically playing in each other's arms. As for me: I relegated myself on top of the beach towel we laid out on the sand. I wasn't too far from the water and I was easily tracking the two love birds as they splashed around in the surf. While Jude flaunted around with his massive frame and we'll defined muscles in his red and black trunks with Sena's impeccable body in her bikini with a strong lower half, I had still worn my white tee shirt with Chuck Norris's face plastered over it. Yeah, I was still into that novelty, I considered it classic. Bite me.

Bottom line was: I wasn't exactly down for the fun those two were having, and the sun was well at its peak of the day. I continued to just sit, leaning back on my arms and staring at them. Until they both started to leave the water and headed directly toward me.

"Gabe!" Jude called out to me as they came closer. "C'mon man, you gotta jump in with us! You won't be having any fun sitting in the sun baking like a potato!"

I gave him a wry, unamused glare, daring him to force me out into the water as both of them walked right up to me.

"Thanks but no thanks, Jude," I told him outright. "I'm actually comfortable just sitting here and relaxing and letting you two have your day."

"Well, you aren't going to get a tan with that shirt on," Sena jokingly said. "Besides, we're here for you as well, Gabe. So c'mon, have some fun!"

I could deny and put Jude down all day like I'd been breathing air. But having Sena beg me to enjoy myself with them had the unfortunate effect of tugging at some old heartstrings that had been vulnerable to her sweet voice and caring attitude. To say no to her was equivalent to slapping Mother Teresa's face. That was an inexcusable sin.

"Fine, you win… Just… Don't gawk too much, yeah?"

I got up, standing in front of them and began taking off my shirt.

"Why would we gawk at you?" Jude said quickly, almost mockingly. "It's not like you've got anything to… Hide…Holy…"

Yup, that was what I had expected from him. Once I took my shirt off and tossed it aside, Jude's and Sena's bewildered expressions had welcomed my sight as I faced them.

"Here I thought I'd bulked up…" Jude muttered.

"You got like this… From all of your training?" Sena asked the million-dollar question.

Jude may have had me beat in mass, but while he was meant to have the body to play football, my body was made for combat. One look and you could see just how developed my musculature had been, from being able to clearly see my abs, to picking out nearly all the muscles of my arm. I had conditioned myself to be agile, strong and lightweight. Too much mass would hamper how quick I wanted to move. Plus I wanted to maintain a certain level of flexibility. After all, you can't make bricks bend. I wasn't jacked like a body builder, but I was the happy medium between that and athletic. Just the right amount of shock value with practicality in mind.

But to put it short: I looked like most girls' dream boy.

"You're gawking…" I said plainly at the both of them.

Hilariously enough, they tried to make up excuses like not being really prepared for what they were to see. Couldn't blame them. What does one really say to a friend who has never truly showed off the body of an Adonis until now? To save them any more personal shame, I clasped both of their shoulders, gave them a smile and assured them that no matter what I looked like, I was still ninety percent Gabriel and ten percent cybernetics. Which, thankfully, earned their laughter.

The day at the beach from that point onward was mostly just us, horsing around in the water, eventually just laying down on our blanket in the sun, collecting what tan we could. Though Sena opted to just wear the hoodie she initially brought over her swimsuit. She didn't tan as well as Jude and I, being fair-skinned and all. Hell, even the occasional girl came around, if only to take vanity shots with me and Jude. Guess we weren't too bad looking after all. Even Sena joked about us being potential models. Which made some of the women that came near us uncomfortably giddy with excitement.

The people with the strangest fantasies, I swear...

After the beach, we decided to hit up a nearby restaurant that plenty of beachgoers often hung out at.

"Well, Gabe, did ya have a good time today or what?" Jude asked with an overly satisfied smile.

I took a sip of soda I'd gotten while we sat at our table, waiting for our dinner. We agreed that afterward, we'd have Jude's dad bring us to his house together and spend the night. Much to my protest, but both of them insisted. Guess they must've thought it'd be better if I had friends nearby if I still had nightmares.

"Fine, I'll admit it," I said with a halfhearted grin. "I had fun with you guys."

Jude and Sena glared at me, calling BS on my admission. I chuckled and tried my best to convince them otherwise. Eventually, I won them over, but wholeheartedly, I did have a good time. It helped take my mind off Elouise for the day, easily keeping my mental health in the green zone. I couldn't express how grateful I'd been for them.

Just as we had gotten our dinner served, a loud crash, followed by the unmistakable discharge of firearms echoed within the restaurant. Not long after, screams.

"Nobody move one goddamn muscle!" A loud, angry man yelled.

I could hear him making some obscene demands like a cliché gunman would. Do this or get shot or do this and get shot. He didn't register to me as much as the terrified faces of Jude and Sena. While Jude did his best to cover her and try to hide themselves from the danger, I hadn't reacted in the same manner.

Instead, I gave them a sly grin and mouthed to them, "Don't worry, I'll handle this."

I rose from my seat and began to search for the gunman that had entered. I eventually caught sight of him, harassing a couple at their table. I moved to a more open area to properly confront him. Didn't want unnecessary collateral damage.

"Hey, jackass!" I called to him with his back turned, antagonizing him intentionally.

He whipped about, aiming his rifle at me, and showing no hesitation, fired a round at me.

No, I didn't dodge like Neo did. For that demanded inhuman reflexes and skills that not a single inch of my body possessed. But my right arm and eye did. The superior reaction and movement of both working in tandem helped block the bullet that would have taken my heart. I didn't allow the bullet to ricochet as my cybernetic hand actually caught it in its palm, negating all the incoming force with ease.

But the gunman wasn't daunted in the slightest, assuming it was just some stroke of luck. He was about to start unloading into me. Sad for him, though, because I began to utilize a special gadget in my palm that acted as a powerful magnet. Simpler explanation: my powers of magnetism just went active.

He squeezed on that trigger so many times as I stuck my arm out lazily, hardly treating him like a threat. During the hailstorm of bullets, I could hear the patrons, and even Sena, cry out in horror. He continued until his gun went empty with a satisfying click. All the bullets he fired had been floating in a ball near my palm, unmoving and completely harmless. Everyone was in awe of what was happening. But then they all began to stare at the schmuck with the empty gun.

I grinned at him amused with a very halfhearted look as I brought my arm closer to me with the ball of rounds. While moving my fingers like I'd been sprinkling some sort of garnish, bullets began to drop from the floating ball to the floor.

"Y'know, I normally don't take pleasure in doing things like this," I finally spoke aloud, treating the man like he was nothing to me as I slowly approached him with a clenched fist. "But, you picked the worst possible day to roll in here with a gun. I was trying to have a good day with my friends, and since I'm already damned to hell, I'm not ready to let something like you ruin it."

I stood right up to the man who was closer to Jude's height at first, but he cowered so far back that he fell flat on his ass. So now I towered over him.

"You tried to shoot me in the chest, right where my heart is," I continued with a deadpan threatening tone, I could see the shivers roll down the spines of everyone else around me. "That meant you were really trying to kill me. So whatever happens to you next is what you deserve, don't you agree?"

He nodded so fast, hoping I'd give him mercy. But for the most part, I wanted him to realize his position and how screwed he was. So, without a further word, I drew my right arm back and shot it into his face, knocking him out on the floor, sprawled out like a dead animal. But it wasn't enough to kill. I was above that. The people around me started clamoring and soon enough, began cheering.

Not exactly how I wanted things to go, but better than the alternative, which was more grisly. Suddenly, I felt Jude wrap his arms around me along with Sena who'd been in tears, telling me how reckless I was being and how glad they were that I was still alive. I felt the old familiar sensation of belonging whilst they held me close, like I actually mattered to them.

I told them I'd handle it. Could they not believe me?

Chapter 8
Promises

Elouise came back home the next day, unscathed to my great relief, but she was livid with me. News of my heroics spread pretty quickly and thanks to her capabilities of keeping tabs on info traffic flowing through cyberspace. So when she burst through the door, she had yelled out my name in anger, and hunted me down to give me an earful about how unnecessarily reckless I had been in confronting a gunman who I learned was mentally unstable.

I explained to her that Jude and Sena had been with me as well, but Elouise quickly disregarded that and continued to berate me, going on to say how terrified she was if I had been hurt. As angry and verbose she was, she didn't shed a single tear despite how visibly upset she'd been.

"If something happened to you when I was gone... What would I do then?" She asked me desperately.

As much as I wanted to apologize, I didn't feel remorse about what I had to do. It was do or let others, or worse, Jude and Sena die. I wasn't about to have that on my conscience, especially when I had the power to do something about it.

"Elouise, I'm sorry, but I was just doing what I do best," I replied.

"What, being a trained killer?"

"Protecting the people I care about."

Elouise looked taken aback, but she knew what I meant. When I had gotten my upgrade from Alexander back then, Elouise was put in danger in order for me to put the arm to the test. At the time, it was a group of men Alexander had put up to the task. Four nameless men who I mercilessly killed in protection of Elouise.

It was the first time she'd seen what I had really become, and how lethal my gun fighting skills were. It'd been so harrowing that she was legitimately frightened of me; she barely recognized me for who I was over what I became.

I reached out to Elouise, grabbing her hand, trying to convince her I wasn't trying to justify using our friends as an excuse to vent my pent up frustrations.

"I… I know… I was just looking forward to seeing you after having been gone," Elouise solemnly said while lowering her head at me. "I wasn't sure what to really think when I heard the news… They weren't scared, were they?"

I smiled and told her that despite the vicious display, Jude and Sena hadn't been frightened of me. After all I truly showed them who I could become and the results of being a secret agent. They also tried it treat me like a hero as a joke when I had spent the night at Jude's. Sena stayed too despite the terror that transpired. Mainly because her parents were actually gone for the weekend, practically entrusting her to Jude.

I swear he had no idea how good he had it.

"Enough about that, what about you?" I quickly shifted the gears, somewhat anticipating her to tell me some wild tale of danger and adrenaline being on her own.

But one look at how quickly her expression went from serene calm to an overcast dread. I wasn't sure if something happened to her. Physically, she was perfectly untouched, but I knew from experience, the mental damage could be far worse.

"Elouise? What kind of mission did Jackson send you on?"

"It wasn't that…" Elouise softly uttered. "I finally understand how it was for you when you first started."

She took my hand and walked us over the couch in our living room, sitting down while still maintaining a firm grasp. Elouise took in a deep breath, gathering her own emotions before she was willing to speak about the experience.

"It wasn't so much the ease of how I completed the mission. I honestly believed it'd be so easy that'd I would be able to brag to you about it… But no. It was worse than I could ever imagine. When you told me about how many people's lives you actually affect and how you managed to keep yourself together somehow, I thought I could do the same…"

Elouise began to tear up with her lips quivering. It was disheartening to see my Elouise hit so hard by what I did so often that it just numbed me to just about anything else. I remember why I really didn't want Elouise by herself out there. Working together with me, she focused on making sure I came back home in one piece. By herself: she'd be thrust into the cruelty and self-loathing carried solely by me until now.

"I tried... I tried keeping low, keeping unnecessary contact to an absolute minimum," Elouise said, struggling to come to terms with the results of her mission I had been far too familiar with. "But even as technologically advanced as I am now, I was just so naive! One thing led to another, and at a certain point, I just... Let go, and activated an auto pilot I configured on the spot, to keep me from doing something beyond stupid. But that didn't keep me from seeing what I inevitably caused..."

She buried her head into my chest, seeking comfort from the man who did it all first. The man who was still just piecing himself back together with glue and duct tape. Truly, who else could she really talk to about this? If Jude or Sena, they'd be at a loss. It'd be unfair to them. Not like I was any better for her, but for now, I was the best she had.

"I really don't know how you do it Gabe... God, look at us now, talking about how we've ruined countless people's lives, ruined families... We shouldn't be talking about this, we should be talking about friends, our day to day lives at school and out of it..."

Elouise wrapped her arms around me and squeezed tightly, expecting me to somehow save her.

"I'm scared, Gabe, I'm scared of losing who I am if this is what's expected of us now. I'm afraid I'll lose everything and everyone I care about, even you! I don't want to be alone..."

That was my ultimate cue, and I didn't hesitate to grab her and hold her closer to me, placing my chin on top of her head, like I was protecting her again.

"You won't ever be alone, I can promise you that," I said with fierce gritty determination.

Elouise brought her head up, removing my head from atop hers to stare shocked at me. Hearing me speak in that manner must've resonated deeply within her as it did myself. I can only recall myself being this strong sounding when I had first made her the promise that so long as I was alive, I wouldn't let anyone take her from me. How cheesy that was, but at the time, it was called for, just like I felt it was now. Just as what I was about to declare next with absolute conviction.

"I know we're still young, but like we talked about before, about our lives being like this, it won't be forever. But at the same time, I want to be with you always. So when the day comes when we're finally free, I want to make that official."

"Gabe… Are you… proposing to me?" Elouise asked.

I smiled playfully in response, making light of her sudden realization as she continued to stare dumbstruck. If it was any more amusing, it would be similar to the day I finally reciprocated her feelings that she held on to, but never truly expressed.

"Kind of, but not yet," I said plainly. "For now, things will have to stay the way they are, for obvious reasons, but what I'm saying is, when we're free, we'll probably be out of high school, at that point I want to ask—"

"Yes," Elouise bluntly answered without having been asked the question, like she was beyond ready to accept my feelings.

"Uh, Elouise? I haven't even asked yet—"

"I don't care. Yes!"

She hugged me tight, tighter than ever before, which unfortunately meant she was ultimately squeezing my chest in so much, it was beginning to become a struggle to breathe normally.

"Elle…Elouise! Can't breathe!"

I tried tapping out but she only maintained her steadfast embrace, becoming the affectionate python.

"Just make sure to keep your promise about being safe, please?" Elouise gingerly asked while loosening her grip.

I grinned happily, but it was more bittersweet, because of how I couldn't truly make good on that promise completely.

"I can't guarantee that, I told you, but I can promise I'll make it back in one piece. Can that work?"

Elouise smooshed her face into my chest again, rubbing it profusely, acting like a child accepting my conditions. So I held her tightly, treating her like the treasure she'd been to me.

It almost felt like how things were before, it'd been so nostalgic. For the first time since her death, she was my world again; my reason for coming back home every day.

Except now we both had that same line of thinking. Whether it was both or just one of us, we just wanted to see each other back home and together. Our only hope was that we wouldn't have to live like this forever.

The next year flew by much quicker than either of us expected, but hadn't been unwelcome. Thanks to my pseudo-marriage proposal, Elouise and I seemingly improved by leaps and bounds in our effectiveness together and on our own whenever Jackson tasked us with our assignments. It was a silent arrangement that we'd do our best to get whatever was needed done and without being injured in the process. And somehow, we were happier for it.

Hell, even Jude and Sena noticed. Especially since we started making more time for dates between us, making the moments matter with each and every fleeting day we had to ourselves not spent at school or somewhere being forced to do demolitions, executions or quick random acts of espionage. It hadn't been more of us becoming too dependent on each other's being, it had been more of a, well a vow. In sickness and in health, until death, do us part.

We still had some inner demons to deal with, Elouise with her cybernetics and the people she used to call her parents and, of course, me with my intermittent nightmares of us revolving around what I did to Elouise. But we continued working through those issues. We weren't about to let them control us forever, even I began learning how to come to terms and forgive myself.

We'd been like strange poster children for maturity, even though the only two who'd ever know why had been Jude and Sena.

Life for us started too seem more normal as things continued, but we were still eager for better times.

On this day, it was normal as most schools go, except now I was driving my own vehicle, a red Jeep of all things. To me, it felt right, having a ride that would handle both asphalt and off-road. Call it being paranoid, but I liked it. Anyway, we met Jude and Sena in the student parking lot of the school, who were getting around by Jude's own car, an old used, but reliable sedan his parents helped him get.

We did as normal teenagers did, we reaffirmed our friendships with hugs and handshakes, joked around before class, talked about potential plans for the week and then made our way to classes when the bell rang. This year, Elouise and I were separated from Jude and Sena at lunch, so we were just sitting together near a tree, sitting in the shade enjoying a lunch, quietly.

We tended to keep to ourselves and just enjoy the physical company of each other, especially when she was in my left arm's grasp and laying into my chest and my head was resting on hers. It was a silent time for us, which somehow got us a picture by a member of the school newspaper club during Valentine's day. We gave them permission, so long as we kept a copy for ourselves. That gave us some notoriety as one of the more recognizable couples in school.

"Mmm... Any plans for dinner tonight, Gabe?" Elouise asked lazily.

"Dunno, Elle, maybe we can just order pizza?"

"Bleh, pizza? That was last week's idea."

"Chinese?"

"Laaaaame! How about Italian?"

"So, pizza?"

"Quit being a smartass, you know what I mean, dummy."

"Haha, I know, couldn't help it. But at that point I might as well make pasta with bread and oil."

"Sounds delish!"

Elouise nuzzled me as she squeezed me tighter, embracing the idea of me cooking up a yummy meal for the two of us. I grinned with satisfied pleasure. Despite the simple exchange, it was just what we liked. Simple, nothing too extreme outside of our actual occupations.

But just as we continued to settle down and sit happily together, my right eye's HUD displayed an alert just as Elouise pulled her head off me, already searching around for the immediate threat.

My HUD displayed a unique warning message, alerting me to cybernetic configuration that wasn't my own, or Elouise's. The only other time I had ever gotten the message was when I had first gotten my arm back in the eighth grade.

Getting this message now meant worse things other than a potential kindred spirit. The worst part was: there was no telling just what exactly it was that came within range, so we weren't sure whether to be ready for combat or have open arms for a potential ally.

But perhaps what made us more uneasy was the fact it was broad daylight at school. Who would be bold enough to stage an attack now of all times and places?

"Gabe, what do we do?" Elouise asked quietly, but it was clear how tense she was, ready to pop off at the first sign of danger. She was still scanning about, trying to locate the potential danger.

"Don't do anything yet, can't risk drawing others into our mess," I warned her, taking note of all the other students around. A recipe for disaster is what we had.

All it would take is a single weapon discharge to send everyone in panic. And an ensuing firefight could be absolutely catastrophic.

While having that thought and scanning around, the sound of what I feared split the air. Elouise immediately grabbed me and put my body flat to the ground. I knew instinctively what she was trying to do and relaxed my body, letting her manipulate me in time to avoid being hit on the tree. When I turned my head while on the ground to see what was fired at me, and what I saw was a charred hole, bored into the trunk of the tree with a bright yellow residue in the center, cooling rapidly. One moment of analysis from my eye told me that a plasma caster had been fired at me. A freaking weapon that equated to a plasma gun from science fiction games in space was fired at me.

"Gabe! On the roof, ten o'clock!"

I shot back up in time to see students around me start to panic and scurry about. When I looked toward Elouise's direction, I saw a figure kneeling with arms raised at us. When the figure realized we could make it out from our position, it didn't flee. It ran toward us and jumped down, landing without so much as receiving any sort of shock through the legs and began advancing quickly, the arms now becoming clear they were transformed into plasma casters. However, the cybernetics were not as sophisticated as Elouise's, looking crude and simple with a glowing core at the elbow and a long barrel with ivory white parts of the arms acting as barrel covers.

Elouise and I still didn't react defensively as we would any other time, but as the figure drew closer, we could see it was female, but something about her face and reddish brown hair were strangely familiar.

We didn't have time to discuss as she fired on us again, except with rapid bursts of plasma, forcing us to leap out of the line of fire. While Elouise dove to the left, I had ran toward a table and used the strength of my right arm to uproot it from the concrete, flipping it into a makeshift cover. Which had some effectiveness as the woman continuously fired on me instead of focusing on Elouise. That told me something critical: she may not have been the real target.

Elouise, you aren't her focus. We may be able to take advantage of that.

You sure? She's closing on you with both arms, and that table won't last much longer!

Let her come closer, then try and take her down. We'll coordinate from there. Keep the link active.

Got it! Please be careful.

Don't have to tell me twice! We'll handle this together!

I prepared myself for close quarters combat, transforming the knuckle portion of my right arm with electrical points. There was something I wanted to confirm.

When the girl came close enough, I heard Elouise slam her directly into my improvised cover, my cue to leap out and grab the girl by her head as Elouise held her from behind. Working in tandem while I was leaving over both of them, we performed the tag team from hell on her.

Elouise let go of her and put some distance between her and the assailant, just in time for me to grab the girl by one of her legs with my cyber arm and tossed her overhead into the floor onto her back.

She didn't make any sort of cry of pain, nor did she truly recoil in pain. The slam I delivered would have easily elicited that much from anyone human. But I managed to take a brief glimpse at the girls face, despite having crude facial plates over her mouth and recognized the cybernetically enhanced green-blue eyes. All in time for receiving a metal plate foot into my chest, knocking me away as she rose back onto her feet, transforming her arms again, this time forming a three blade circular saw for her hands. She'd been dressed like a normal teenager like us, with tee shirt and jeans that had been ruined by her cybernetic leg plates. It was almost reminiscent of when Elouise and I last saw her, but we swore she was dead.

Ariel Tessa stood before us once again. A girl I had once promised to help find answers about her family.

Gabe, this isn't possible, right? That can't be her, is it?

Does it look like an illusion? Or do you believe in ghosts? That's definitely her. No doubt about it.

But why was she attacking us?

She didn't give me enough time to think it over clearly as she lunged directly at me with her saw blades spinning quick enough to make me feel the air whoosh past my face as I managed to dodge her saw blade strikes. I reacted in kind with a quick right jab into her stomach, jolting her body with a burst of twenty-thousand volts and enough force to knock her back ten feet.

Do a quick scan on her, Elouise. I'll keep her busy, she seems overly fixated on me.

It won't take long, just—

Be careful, right?

Now's not the time, Gabe! Just don't get careless!

I rushed at Ariel, keeping my arms raised in a defensive posture. Before we engaged again, I brought my arm to my left and encased all of my left forearm with cybernetic armor plating, a trick I came up with when Elouise and I were surrounded at one point by gangsters with knives. Ariel came at me again, aiming for my chest, but I easily deflected her saw blades with my right arm and landed a left hook into her head, despite the enhancement, my left-handed punch didn't have the same driving force as my right arm, so it only made a glancing blow to Ariel's head. Thankfully, my right hand was fast enough to follow up almost immediately, driving its palm into her face, opening up to reveal a large bore tube. After being staggered back, a thick smokescreen poured out of my arm, quickly expanding and enveloping the immediate area of our fight.

Gabe, she's being controlled. There's programming overriding her consciousness, like how it was with me.

Can we free her?

It's no problem from me, but I'll have to make a direct connection to her.

Which means I have to disable her, right?

No one said just you, but yeah, in a nutshell. But thanks to that smokescreen of yours, I've got an idea. Electrify it.

The idea sent shivers down my spine. Because she knew the smokescreen was laden with the arm's nanomachines. And she'd seen what I had done with them before, she knew how lethal they could be. For her to suggest electrifying the entire cloud with Ariel still inside, made me worry she still held a grudge against her. More on that later…

For now, a high enough level of voltage would be enough to at least immobilize her. Without another moment wasted, I punched out at the smokescreen, discharging electrical currents from my knuckles through the air and into the cloud of nanomachines. The resulting display was like a miniature lightning cloud before us with flashes of blue tinted light. As instant as it was, it halted quickly.

Elouise rushed into the cloud with no hesitation, eager to get to Ariel. Meanwhile all around us, we had unwittingly drew the attention of a crowd of students, all now interested in what just happened. Made me beyond grateful Elouise and I mastered the art of non-vocal communication through our cyber link up.

Gabe, I've terminated the programming controlling Ariel.

Good, get her out of here. Go around back and fly her off.

To where?

Where else? Home. I'll meet you there.

Elouise didn't argue, this wasn't the time or place. Besides, just as I had questions behind her reappearance, I was sure Elouise had the same ones. Why did she come back, why only target me? Did Elouise's cover get blown, who else knew, why so desperate? So much to ask, but not here.

Once I made sure Elouise had cleared the smokescreen, I raised my arm and retrieved all of the airborne nanomachines and hurried off to my Jeep, leaving behind plenty of stunned students, but not a single faculty member would stop me or even show concern, as to be expected.

Just what the hell was going on?

Chapter 9
Release

When Gabe told me who this girl was that I flew in my arms like a sleeping princess back home with, I couldn't believe it. There was so much time between what happened when Gabe first met her and now. If Gabe wasn't sure she was, then I was one hundred percent positive Ariel has died.

Back in middle school, when Gabe had first moved away, Ariel had entered my life, innocently enough. But as time quickly passed, she found herself on my bad side, almost instantly. That had been due to her manipulating me into hacking the school's administration system, just to change a couple of grades, what pissed me off is after the fact and how mad and disappointed in myself for having listened to her and having done something so illegal.

My only saving grace there was the fact I was so good at hacking, no one would have known it was me, that and I was still just an unassuming kid. But I did deal with Ariel, pretty much telling her I didn't want to so much as see or talk to her ever again. Kind of like how I did my parents, but at middle school standard. No gunfire involved there. To me Ariel was some conniving weasel that wanted to take advantage of me and my skills. No telling what else she would have wanted.

Then Gabe came back and after I gave him his arm, he and Ariel interacted in ways I didn't want him to, ways I feared would have terrible ramifications, which got me pissed off at him as well as her. It was only until I found out that Gabe was actually helping Ariel did I learn that she was cybernetically modified by her birth parents when she was a baby. She grew up under a foster family that had been on the payroll of the Atlas group, the company her parents were a part of and had been technology research and development. When I dug deeper, I found they were desperate to make some new technology to compete with my parent's company that had been driving them into the ground in that field.

Then that night, while taking a walk to the store nearby our home, we ran into her, being chased by armed men in Black SUV's. We got caught up in the shootout between her and thanks to her selfless act of engaging them outright, we managed to sneak off without being seen. It was one of the few things we told Jude and Sena about our lives before Gabe became the secret soldier. All four of us agreed to never speak of what happened to Ariel, especially since there was no news or chatter about what transpired that night, almost like it never happened.

Yet, here she was again in my life. When I brought her into our home, I laid her on the couch in the living room, placing her in a comfortable position on her back. I took another moment to take a scan of her body. While much of her cybernetics had been recognizable from that night, it appeared someone tried upgrading her, albeit crudely. Her tech was still leagues behind my own, and only had access to a small limited amount of constructs, but plenty had been changed. Even some of her internal organs had been replaced to emplace artificial parts to further improve her performance. What good it did her against me and Gabe. But I felt my own makeshift heart drop into my stomach.

The only people I could think of who would do this, had been her parents. I pitied her for it. How could someone do this to their own flesh and blood? It wasn't even to protect her as for their own personal gain. Absolutely, deplorably selfish. They'd been on their own tier of scum my parents couldn't reach.

"Oh Ariel, I wish you had told me sooner, I could have helped you more…" I muttered while observing her resting body.

She began to stir seemingly in response to my solemn, apologetic words of pity. Ariel's eyes slowly open, taking in the surroundings she'd been placed in. She wasn't startled at first, until she turned her gaze upon me.

"Who… Who are you?" She spoke for the first time, her small voice quivering in fear.

Of course, she wouldn't recognize me completely. It'd been a few years sure, but my appearance was definitely not what she would have easily remembered. I gently grabbed her shoulders, smiling at her to calm her down.

"It's alright now, Ariel. You're safe here. I'm Elouise, remember? I know I look different, but a lot has changed since you saved us that night."

Her eyes shot wide in realizing who was talking to her and almost immediately shooting her entire body into mine, hugging me tightly like I was the lost child. Ariel began crying profusely while holding on to dear life.

The door from the hallway leading into the garage opened and closed quickly, letting me know Gabe had made it home. When he saw us two hugging it out, he kept quiet until Ariel investigated the new presence in the room. When she saw it was Gabe smiling down on her, she continued to tear up in my arms, professing how glad she was to see us again.

After a few minutes of her letting out all of her emotions, we sat on the couch and told her what had been happening that led to her being in our home. That ultimately led to the real questions for her to answer if she could.

"Why were you attacking us? Who sent you?" Gabe asked.

I listened intently, less like an interrogator but as someone who just wanted to know what she did.

"Who else but my parents," she replied instantly, but with a notable tone of disdain. "Those assholes installed that programming in me when they had me collected, just so they could control me without worrying I'd be a liability."

I took a quick glance over to Gabe, with my expression of wonder, I silently said "here I thought I had issues." To which Gabe simply gave a bemused look, almost taking pleasure in the moment.

"Honestly though, those losers had nothing left to offer Atlas," Ariel continued scathingly regarding her parents. "They just couldn't come up with anything to compete with Elouise's parents. I was their last resort. They figured they could use me to get Gabriel's arm and bring it back on the premise they could manage something from it. I may have been a slave but I was still conscious, so I knew everything that'd been going on. So I knew they had no chance in hell of using that arm to save their hides. The other companies had already set sail from those plans when Elouise's death was made public. By now my parent's work may as well be canned and done with."

Those last words put me and Gabe into a state of disbelief. I was wide-eyed, still trying to take in what I had just heard from Ariel, who may have been our ultimate savior again.

"Hold on, what did you say? The other companies have backed off? For how long?" Gabe asked quickly, anxious to hear the answer to the question we had both been looking forward to since he started working.

Ariel looked at both at us and realized the massive importance of her words. She went on to explain that it'd been months since everyone involved that held a special interest in me in the past had moved on, decidedly dropping out of the tech race for good.

I glanced over to Gabe who had a very powerful, serious glare in his eyes.

"I'll be back, I've got to make a call," he said before leaving the room into the foyer.

"So, I know what I said when I mentioned you were dead, but obviously, you're not," Ariel said to me, catching my attention. When I looked back to her, she'd been extremely curious with how I had managed to fool everyone she knew about.

"What's really going on here, Elouise?" She asked.

I brought it upon myself to tell her the truth, I felt I owed her that much in spite of how I already saved her once. But thanks to her words, this would be the second way I could reciprocate her actions, even if she didn't really know it.

So I told her what had happened to me, how Gabriel was forced by the people he now worked for, to include my parents, to murder me and then have me turned into a cyborg under an alias. The world was fooled by a very lame, but convincing cover up orchestrated by Gabriel's boss.

By the time I finished telling her my part of the much bigger story, she was clasping her hands over her mouth with horror all over her fair-skinned face.

"Gabe... is still haunted by what happened in his dreams, but," I continued, but smiling to reassure Ariel that we hadn't let what happened sour things between us. "He's been improving over the months, I believe he's getting closer to forgiving himself when before he felt like he deserved to die. He's stronger now, I know that for sure. He may never forget, but he won't let it bog him down forever."

And that's why I still love him. He pushes through the toughest crap no kid should even be presented with. He may get cuts and bruises, but he's managed to come out in one piece.

Ariel's horror began to fade into calm and then admiration. Somehow, I felt she was happy for us. Despite all the crap we'd been subjected to, we were still close. If only she knew.

Gabriel entering from the foyer drew our attention to him, and he was beaming with such an elated expression, I was sure we'd somehow won the lottery, but I already had a feeling of what we actually won, it just hadn't hit me yet the reality of that hunch.

I left Ariel and Elouise on the couch together as I walked off. With my arm, I placed a headset onto my ear and called Jackson. Unsurprisingly, he had answered almost immediately, telling me how "ironic" that he was about to call me all the same. I was no longer willing to play his game anymore.

"Cut the shit, Jackson," I said angrily but quietly to not to draw the girls' attention. "Tell me something, how long has it been since it's been safe for Elouise? How long has it been since those rival groups decided to ditch the gold mine?"

Silence. I pressured him more, telling him it didn't matter if he lied, what I knew now was enough to never listen to another order ever again.

"Alright, alright, I'll tell you," he said quickly, realizing it was futile at long last. "It's been eleven months, almost immediately after Elouise's death."

"And how long were you planning on sitting on that, huh?"

"Gabriel, please understand, you two were invaluable assets. We couldn't just let you go when there was so much more good you can do!"

"Oh blow me, your idea of 'good' was nothing more than people dying left and right. Even when we weren't tasked with actual killing. If someone so much as laid eyes on us, you silenced them without a moment's notice! Well that all ends now. I just wanted to call you so I can hear you say it."

"Gabriel?"

"Say it. 'Gabriel, you aren't required to complete any further assignments, and by extension, neither will Elouise.' Say it."

Jackson hesitated silently, but he knew I finally had him dead to rights.

So I pressed him even further.

"There is no threat to protect us from anymore. Face it, we're through working for you. You've got nothing on us to really use. And if you expose us, Elouise can bury you all the same. That'd be awkward, wouldn't it?"

"Fine! You've made your point!"

"So say it!"

Jackson finally repeated the words I had said, word for word. And it felt satisfying to hear him groveling as he said it.

"And one last thing. I never want to hear or see you ever again. Goodbye."

I hung up without giving him an opportunity to respond. Just as I wanted. This was the victory I've always wanted. For almost three years we've been robbed of our lives, our innocence. Starting today, we take it back.

I walked over to the living room, just in time to hear Elouise end her talk with Ariel, just as she finished telling her how I'd been doing with my skeletons. But I knew the underlying meaning of her words. And I loved her for being with me this far. It made my chest feel weightless.

When the girls finally noticed I was in the room, I kept smiling at Elouise who was waiting for the words she may as well have been waiting to hear come out of my mouth.

"Gabe?" She called anxiously.

"We're free, Elle, we're finally free," I said with such a proud and gentle voice, it gave even me shivers down my spine.

Elouise let those words sink in gradually, letting it all flow into her as she slowly rose from the couch and walked over to me. Elouise kept staring deeply into my eyes, to find any sort of doubt, any reason to believe what I had just said may have been false. But I guess she never did as she grabbed me and squeezed tightly, relieved of her own worries and fears as she burrowed her face into my shoulder.

"Then… Then that means we can finally just be you and me?"

I embraced her just as tight, finally feeling like I was home for good.

"You said it. There's nothing to threaten us anymore. Nothing to make us slaves to Jackson."

We stood there in the moment, no longer caring about anything else but us. It'd been too long since I could have the privilege of saying I could be a normal kid living a typical average life. And too long has it been since Elouise and I have gotten together and actually have a normal relationship. Our lives were screwed up the night we accepted each other's feelings and started "dating". Now that it was over, we could have what Jude and Sena had.

"Uh, I hate to ruin the moment," Ariel chimed in, reminding us we hadn't really been alone. "But what the heck has been going on? What do you mean by 'free'?"

Elouise and I broke apart, starting at Ariel, only to break into a small laugh, realizing she wasn't in the loop.

"I don't know what Elle has told you, but there's a lot you missed since you were gone."

"Well, I've got nowhere to go in a hurry. Elouise told me her part of the story, so I'm all ears to yours."

After taking seats on the couch again, I began retelling her the story of us so far until today, and by the end of it all, Ariel was crying silently. She remarked that she didn't know who had it worse anymore, her or us.

We told her she didn't have to compare our lives to hers, on a certain level, we three have had our own hells to experience. Ultimately Ariel wanted to blame herself, believing because of what happened that night might've exposed the two of us. But I reassured her it was nothing like that when I had learned Elouise had been targeted long before.

After a little while of me and Elouise assuring Ariel things were okay between us and there wasn't any fault on her, Ariel asked the important question.

"So, what are you two going to do with me?"

Elouise and I looked at each other briefly, but knew already what we wanted to do.

"Isn't it obvious, Ariel?" I said looking back to her worried face. "You can stay here with us. As long it's okay with Elle."

"Hey, you should be asking Ariel that. I've got no problem letting her stay here."

Ariel looked shocked and speechless. It took her a minute before she could deliver a response.

"Why?"

Again, Elouise and I smiled at her.

"Because you saved us. Twice. This is the least we owe you, after all, you don't exactly have anywhere else to go, right? Not like you've got family to trust."

She shrugged with a blank face, unable to disagree.

"But… is this really okay with you guys?"

"Do we have to repeat ourselves here?"

At that point, Ariel shut up and leapt at us, grabbing us in her arms and hugging us together like a sandwich. She repeatedly thanked us between sobs she'd been holding back, finally coming to terms with her feelings about staying.

Truth be told, she really didn't have anyone she could trust other than us and as far anyone knew, she didn't really exist. Elouise and I let Ariel continue hugging us while we conversed messages through our cyber link up. Discussing her new room, which would be my old one, and what next to do.

Do we tell Jude and Sena about this? Elouise asked.

They'll find out sooner or later, but we've no reason to hide her. We'll call them tomorrow. It's been a long day for us, and I think Ariel deserves some rest.

Good idea since it's the weekend, and maybe I can look over her tech. She may have been "upgraded" but it's all horribly misconfigured. Her parents rushed her cybernetics so much that it could have bad repercussions on her organic parts.

Haha, well, she'll definitely have a good time with you poking around. Just don't mess her up too bad.

Who do you think I am? You forget I'm still an expert in this field and with my body now? There isn't a damn thing I can't accomplish!

With that, I knew Ariel would be in good hands. Though I wasn't entirely sure about the future ahead now. Whatever lay ahead would definitely not have anything more to do with more death and misery. Never again.

Chapter 10
The Elephant in the Home

I called Jude that night to see if he and Sena could meet up with us the next day at the mall. He made sure they could and would. He didn't bother asking if Elouise and I were okay as it had been a silent agreement that, when it concerned the two of us, we'd be okay even if a bomb threat was made. Given our track record, it was a given if either one if us was threatened in public, Jude or Sena would have to call emergency for the offending party.

When we met up with them the next day, we arrived early, to surprise them with Ariel. Elouise didn't just giver her cybernetics an overhaul, but even provided her clothes that were a perfect fit, as they both shared a similar size. We had been sitting in the food court area, our typical meet up spot at the mall and waited patiently while Ariel was twiddling her fingers, anxious to meet them as well. Elouise and I teased her about it, making light that she wasn't completely prepared for meeting more familiar faces that hadn't a good interaction with her. She barked back that she was bracing herself for whatever they had to say, only to hear us tell her it'll be fine, and that those two weren't one to hold grudges.

It wasn't long before those two eventually arrived. And the very first thing I heard from Jude was: "Holy crap... Is that..."

Ariel, who was sitting across from me and Elouise was sitting facing Jude and Sena when they found us. It was impressive that he could recognize her, despite only being three years.

"Ariel?" Sena said next, practically finishing Jude's sentence.

"Take a seat, guys, there's a good story here to tell," I told them, breaking their shock.

We told them what exactly happened at school the day before, and afterward, Ariel told her side of the story for all of us to hear. Turned out, when she was captured three years ago, she wasn't killed for having gone back to her foster home and killing her caretakers for having decided her. Instead, they decided to lock her up, but they didn't toss the key.

Ariel's parents had invested so much time and money into her, they couldn't afford to simply destroy her. Instead they tried upgrading her, trying to improve on what could only have been described by Elouise as cheap ten year old's enhancements. In simpler terms, they sucked and they could barely improve her. What resulted was a body that was becoming more machine than human.

And after our violent reunion, Elouise fixed her up and even replaced parts with creations she whipped up in her workshop overnight. Thanks to her cybernetics, she didn't require the normal quota for rest and sleep. The same could be said for Ariel, but as it was discovered, the efficiency of her cybernetics had been taxing her actual body, so when

Elouise was fixing her up, she'd fallen asleep on the workshop table within moments of laying down.

Jude and Sena could not express their pity anymore with how they looked at Ariel. While she herself wore a solemn and bittersweet smile, Jude was at a loss while Sena was predictably tearing up in hearing the horror that was Ariel's life.

"And it's safe for her to be here?" Jude asked. "I know you guys said her parents and other groups have backed off you all, but what about her?"

"Don't sweat it," I confidently declared. "Atlas is the very least of our worries, since they have put her parents down the drain."

"Beyond them," Elouise chimed in. "I sincerely doubt anyone would even consider anything that was made by Atlas. No offense Ariel."

Ariel giggled, silently agreeing with the point of fact. Not that she'd be completely insulted by Elouise's making clear her parents were not only terrible, but had been comparably inept against Elouise.

"So why bring her here other than surprising us?" Sena asked.

"Glad you asked! See, Ariel's going to be living with us from now on, but as it stands she's wearing Elouise's clothes. So we figured why not take her shopping? Hope you don't mind, it's one of the reasons I had called Jude to see if you could come, too."

Sena took a quick look at Ariel, realizing her clothes had been in fact the same ones Elouise once wore. She then smiled at Elouise in a way I hadn't seen before. It was the smile of a girl who'd just found the perfect moment to simply go wild.

Sena didn't speak a single word when she shot up from her seat, grabbed Elouise and Ariel and then told Jude and I to have fun by ourselves. To which both of us had stared blankly at Sena, now with the bewildered girls in tow, as she gave us a very unsettling glare, telling us she was in charge now, and that we should listen or else.

After she left, it continued to be a shock to me seeing this side of Sena. I looked to Jude for some reassurance that this was merely a fluke. But one look at his defeated grin told me all I needed to know. I only knew Sena as far as a friend could, but Jude had known her as his girlfriend, and with such an intimate relationship, he knew that deep down, Sena had the capacity to be something frightening.

I took the silent exchange of information for what it was worth. For as far as I knew Sena, at least I knew Ariel was in good hands. So, just as Sena suggested, Jude and I simply started walking about, at first asking more about the situation with me and Elouise no longer forced to do missions ever again, but we lightened the mood with old stories from years past. Happier moments in time. But that mood soon soured over with Jude's sudden question.

"So what are going to do with Ariel?" He asked as if I hadn't already made clear my intention.

"I told you, didn't I? She's going to live with us."

"Let me rephrase that. What are you going to do when Ariel starts getting too close to you?"

The question left me still confused, but agitated as I slowly pieced together what he meant by his words.

"The hell, Jude? Why is that a concern?"

"Call it an inferred observation," he continued while we walked. "From what you've told us about her, she may not see you and Elouise clearly as a couple. Not only that, but the last three years of her life, hell even before then, I doubt had been anything but normal development. In other words, Gabe, she may not have the same level of maturity as you and Elouise. Understand what I'm getting at?"

I hadn't expected Jude to come at me with such a well thought-out explanation, especially over Ariel, that it frightened me. Mainly because he had made a cruelly true statement of fact. Ariel hadn't grown up like us. She was either being monitored by her fake family, or she was subjected to technological experimentation. She never once had a normal life until today.

"I don't mean to say it's not a good idea to let her live with you guys, but I'm saying make it clear for her to understand. You and I both know Elouise's temper can get explosive. God forbid something happens with Ariel and she goes ballistic."

I sighed heavily and the pain of having my shoulder stabbed radiated from where Elouise had done so. She may have done a bang-up job patching me up, but the scar was ever present. But only now does it actually feel pain.

"I'll... talk to her when we get back..." I said, dreadfully anxious while lowering my head.

Jude placed his hand on my shoulder, giving me reassurance that it wasn't the worst thing to think about. I wanted to think that, too. But with so much that's happened between me and Elouise, to finally be free to be normal as possible, I was afraid this would be the spark to the powder keg.

As much I would have talked more about how to speak to Ariel, Jude's phone rang. It was Sena telling us she was done with taking Ariel shopping. Luckily, I knew Elouise was paying for the clothes and whatever else they bought for Ariel.

We made our way to the girls, silently. The earlier exchange had my mind racing with ideas of the best and worst case scenarios. But once we caught view of the girls, all of that disappeared when I saw Ariel in her own brand new outfit that made her more like a teenage fashion model with I imagine were the latest trends. Ariel was ecstatic with her new clothes that she ran up to me and did a smooth twirl, showing herself off, asking for my opinion on how she looked. Elouise and Sena had been behind her, with Elouise carrying the bulk of the merchandise she'd bought.

Tell her she looks great! We spent like an hour picking those out!

An hour for clothes?

And other things, too. We got a new bed for her that'll arrive tomorrow afternoon. Among other things. Now tell her!

"You look amazing Ariel," I said smiling without hesitation. But man did my mind suddenly go haywire.

Come the hell on, man. Jude finished telling you to be cautious with her! What're you doing telling her she's amazing?

No one could tell I was mentally berating myself as Ariel smiled gleefully with flushed cheeks. And without warning was hugging me tightly. While the girls didn't seem too bothered, I was losing my mind. With Jude next to me, he had shot me a disapproving look, obviously irritated that after explaining to me that I should take care of the issue with Ariel, here I was already screwing up both in his eyes and in my own mind.

As everyone continued on like normal, talking about the price of the obviously expensive merchandise, I'd been more beside myself, thinking about what to really do, so I hadn't paid much attention to the conversation after Elouise explained despite having disowned her family, they still thought they'd earn her good graces by still sending money every month to her bank account.

Eventually, our day came to an end and we went our separate ways on home. On the drive back, Elouise had been delivering messages to me, asking me if I was okay. She was quick to catch on that I wasn't acting normally as I would with Jude and Sena. But instead of telling her the truth, I lied to her, messaging her that I was just thinking about our future, and got caught up so much on it that I wasn't entirely there at the mall. Elouise bought it, as she had no other reason to believe I could be thinking about worse things anymore.

Now, all I could think of before getting home was how badly she would want to endlessly punch me for lying. It wouldn't be the first time, but it'd hurt no less.

When we finally got home and carried all of the clothes into the house, I thought about what Jude had said. As Ariel and Elouise headed upstairs to store her clothes, I had every intention to stop Ariel and let Elouise go alone. But I didn't. After everything Jude had said, I chose not to say a damn thing.

I was too scared, too afraid to admit there were risks to having someone like Ariel live under the same roof as me.

I chose to go on blind faith that she'd see me and Elouise as the couple who were faithful to each other and understand that there was no place for any excessive displays of affection.

I walked into the kitchen, already losing my thoughts over what to cook for dinner. A distraction to detract from another. That's all it was.

The house was calm and quiet the rest of the day. Not a single disturbance or incident to ruin the time we spent watching TV. For a while, it almost felt like we'd been a family. Albeit a tragic one, but we were making the best of it now. Elouise was sitting on top my lap, leaning softly into my chest as I held her loosely with my arms. Ariel was just next to us, happily enjoying her own freedom.

But as we sat there, I could feel her glances at us. We hadn't explicitly noticed, but I didn't have to turn my head. It'd been one of those sensations you'd feel whenever you feel like you were followed. You knew it was happening, even if there was no one there.

And so I kept lying to myself: it was nothing.

Chapter 11
A Wound and a Twist

The weeks that passed by had all been some of the most blissfully normal time Elouise and I have ever had. When things finally died down from Ariel's return, our daily routine became more predictable and enjoyable. Every morning, we'd get up, have breakfast and get ready for school while leaving Ariel behind at the house. It was Elouise's idea that she'd be better off not leaving the home on the off chance someone recognizes her. Ariel of course expressed her discontent of being kept sheltered up, but couldn't exactly argue with Elouise.

While Ariel was left alone at home, Elouise and I went about our days like normal teenagers. As normal as I believed anyways. Before we settled down, it dawned on us pretty quickly how frighteningly normal our old lives felt when all we'd worry about was when and if we were to be sent out on some mission. Thanks to Jude and Sena being our mental foundation, they reminded us we didn't have to worry about that life anymore. We had said so ourselves, we were free. Eventually, things did go into a normal state where the four of us would meet in the morning in the parking lot to talk, joke and maybe make plans for the weekend.

When the school day was over, home life was even more peaceful as Elouise and I finished up whatever homework that was assigned, I'd cook dinner and Ariel would just chime in with ideas for what to watch on TV. It was one of several things she did to pass time at home. Other than that, she cleaned around the house as best as she could and would surf the net to learn all that she could, since getting her to school was more or less impossible for her.

As for the cleaning, she didn't want to just be a bum in our home, especially since we, and I mean Elouise, bought her clothes, a dresser, bedding and other necessities for her new room. We agreed it was fine for her to do this much, but I honestly felt like I was taking advantage of her like she was a free maid. Albeit with cybernetic enhancements. Weird for most, normal for us.

One Saturday, Elouise went out with Sena for a girls' day out and said she'd be back in time for dinner. Jude had been busy for the weekend so that just left me and Ariel alone in the home. I was fine with that. If anything, I would just laze on the couch and watch TV with Ariel until Elouise came home.

It was that day I learned that Ariel really loved romance movies. Since most of her time was spent in the house, she used streaming services from our TV to watch plenty of movies. Today she wanted to watch Romeo and Juliet with me, the rendition that cast Leonardo DiCaprio as Romeo. She had told me she'd seen it before, but she liked it a lot, having been a classic Shakespeare play with a modern twist to it. Before she started watching it she talked about the tragedy that was the romance between the main characters and how she felt it had been the worst kind of situation to have, but at the same time she admired Romeo and Juliet. To not only recognize they are of rival families but to remain in love with each other, even when they died.

When she asked me of my opinion on it, I simply said I respected rather than admired Romeo. Despite the feud between families, Romeo really loved Juliet, going as far to have the secret marriage. Course I also remarked on how things when downhill when he took revenge for his friend's death at the hands of Juliet's brother. If course I admired Juliet's plan for them to be together without their families meddling ever again, if only the message sent to Romeo had been clearer. That part I believed was the true tragedy of their romance that was doomed. When Elouise and I watched it before, she teared up when Romeo had reached Juliet's seemingly lifeless body and just as she woke up after he drank some poison, we could see the moment where his expression turned to horror and regret.

As Ariel played the movie, she asked me what I'd do if I was in that situation, to which I asked her to be clearer. She then rephrased it, putting me and Elouise in the spotlight. I told her if we were really put in the same series of events, more or less it'd be the same. That was how the story played out. It seemed to bother her that I said it like that, so then she asked if she was Juliet and I was Romeo.

I was confused by that one heavily. I wasn't sure what to say to Ariel at the moment and she could see clearly on my face I wasn't sure about what to say, so she quickly dismissed it, calling it a dumb and stupid question.

After the movie was done, it was around dinner time, so I made my way over to the kitchen to get all the things ready. After watching Romeo and Juliet, I was in the mood for something Italian, but simple. I was sure even Ariel would appreciate it.

I heard her approach me from behind as I was firing up the stovetop. She hugged me from behind, which wasn't all that concerning to me. At this point, it was normal for me and Elouise to get hugs from her like this.

"Gabe, I know I've said this more than enough, but I just wanted to thank you so much for everything," Ariel said softly into my back.

"Aw geeze, Ariel," I said endearingly, accepting her grateful gesture. "You know it was the least we could do for you. You saved us. Pretty sure we've told you that over and over again."

"I know but I still feel like I still owe you."

Her face was flushed. Ariel stared at me longingly as she crept closer to me, placing her hands onto my shoulders, gripping gently.

"Ariel, what're you doing?"

"Paying you back for everything…"

She was a couple inches shorter, but she closed the gap between, standing on her toes to lock her lips with mine. I was confused and mortified. In this seemingly timeless moment, I was trapped and I didn't know how to make any sense of what was going on. Then Jude's warning echoed in the back of my mind.

I shoved Ariel away, backing myself against the stove, damn near getting myself caught on the burners. So I decided to preemptively shut the stove off while never losing sight of Ariel, who looked more hurt by me rejecting her advances.

"Ariel, what the hell?" I said flabbergasted.

She still stared at me, confused. Like she'd expected me to just go along with whatever she had played out in her mind.

"I was just trying to repay you for saving me," she proclaimed as the truth. "I don't have anything else to give, and I've seen from the Internet the best way I could was to give you my body."

It slowly dawned on me that whatever idea Ariel had conceived, she was convinced it had been acceptable. It wasn't so much Ariel wanted to make advances on me, it had been her lack of actual upbringing. She didn't know what had been the acceptable norm. Years of her life robbed and used like a tool, she never grew up learning from a loving family. All she's had were fake foster parents, her cybernetics and the actual parents that had modified her beyond human ethics.

"I mean, I won't lie, I do like you, but in this case, I felt it was the only real way—"

"Ariel, stop, this isn't how things work," I stopped her with a quick hand on her shoulder.

"But I just wanted to repay you…"

"That's not how you do that! You don't just kiss someone and say it's alright! If everything was easily settled like that then…" My voice trailed off when out the corner of my eye, I saw Elouise standing in the kitchen, having just returned.

But she was trembling in fury, her fists clenched like sledgehammers. I finally noticed that my HUD had shown she'd linked up with me around the time I had finished watching the movie with Ariel.

Shit…

I grabbed Ariel and dragged her around, placing myself between me and Elouise.

"Elouise, I can explain," I said keeping my right arm raised, but kept in its normal form.

In response, Elouise snapped both her arms down, instantly transforming her arms into bladed forms, glowing bright blue, radiating energy that was meant to give her blades intense hear to cleave through anything.

"You've got ten seconds to start," she threatened viciously, targeting Ariel behind me.

Elouise didn't have to go through me to get to Ariel. Having always been more lethal and much faster than me, I stood no chance. So I had to speak quickly.

"It's all a misunderstanding, believe me, Ariel doesn't know any better."

"Really? You think I'm going to buy that load of crap?"

"Elouise! Trust me! I'll take care of this! I promise!"

That seemed to halt her fury as she met my eyes in cold, unrelenting anger.

"I'm going outside. And when I come back in, she'd better be gone. You have thirty minutes."

Elouise marched off through the sliding door into the yard, staring at the wall that separated the other yards from ours. I'd managed to buy time, but she didn't have to tell me Ariel wasn't going to stay any longer.

I turned to face her, seeing her frightened like the grim reaper had arrived to take her soul.

"W-why was she so angry? What did I do?"

I pitied her. She truly had no understanding of what she did and just how much danger she was currently in. If I didn't stop Elouise, I had no doubt she'd have her way with Ariel, systematically taking her apart before disposing her body. And no one would really know since by all accounts, Ariel never existed.

I grabbed her hand and dragged her with me to, up to her room. Along the way, she kept begging me to know what was wrong and why Elouise looked like she was ready to kill her. At least she caught on to that much. I could only tell her that she could no longer live with us. I grabbed several sets of her clothes and grabbed a suitcase to throw them in. Ariel was still bewildered by what was happening.

When I took her back down, handing her the suitcase at the door, she grabbed my hand and asked what was she going to do if I was really kicking her out. She had no one to go to other than Jude and Sena, and I wasn't about to throw her on them, especially since doing that carried even more risk to them and their families if they kept her. There was only one thing I could do for Ariel at this point.

I rushed to grab a napkin from the kitchen, bringing it back to Ariel. With my hand, I pressed the napkin into my palm which made a series of tiny holes that made a certain phone number in it then thrusted it into Ariel's hand.

"Call this number in the next hour. He may be a jackass, but he's good for his word. He'll be able to help you."

"Will I ever see you again?" Ariel asked anxiously, desperate to have some sort of reassurance this wasn't permanent.

I closed my eyes, biting my lip, trying not to drag this on any longer.

"When you get older and you understand everything, maybe we'll see each other again. Now go!"

I pushed her on, turning my back to her. I refused to watch her go, even before I walked back into my home and slammed the door. Whatever happened now was on her. She could go anywhere, but this place was no longer her home. And it pissed me off that it had come to this. Mainly because I had ignored Jude's warning.

I had gone and arrogantly believed things would be fine, that Ariel wouldn't do something like this, that she'd understand I was faithful to Elouise. I had screwed up. More for her.

"She's gone, right?" Elouise's voice called to me from the kitchen.

I took notice of her as she stood with her arms to her side, fully reverted. But I had expected her to have them crossed. I was dead sure she was equally pissed off at me.

"She's gone. You won't ever see her again."

"Did you know this would happen?"

I silently nodded.

"Jude had warned me. I chose to ignore it on faith that Ariel knew better…"

Elouise walked toward me, and instead of taking a swing at me, grabbed my hands, holding them gently with an unexpected calm expression.

I get it. You wanted to believe in her like you did before.

So why do I still feel I'm the terrible person?

Elouise pulled me into her embrace, hugging me tight.

"Because that's the man you are," she said sweetly. "Even if you screw up, you try your best, even if it hurts you in the end."

Her time as Raven had been a testament to the fact. Even afterward, I had been trying to do what was right. Even if I got shot, stabbed or punched.

I grasped Elouise's body and held it close to me as I buried my face into her shoulder for comfort. I wasn't crying, but I still felt like even after all this time, I was still falling short, and of course, the one person I believed would hold it against me the most was the one person who was always by my side. Always giving me too much for how much I'd done.

"I'm sorry, Elle," I professed into her shoulder. "I'm just an idiot…"

"You're my idiot, remember?" Elouise playfully said with a giggle. "No matter what, we'll get through anything together."

We stood there for a moment before I had a thought about the entire situation.

"We'll… probably have to tell Jude and Sena about this, won't we?" I asked nervously.

"Yup," Elouise said almost immediately.

"Jude is probably going to take a jab at me, won't he?"

"You deserve it."

"Haha… Great…"

The Monday morning meeting up with Jude and Sena was as expected. We told them what happened with Ariel, and Jude gave me a chance to brace myself before hitting me in the gut, calling me a hopeless idiot as a friend would.

But, in spite of the massive shortcoming, they all assured me my heart had been in the right place, I was just too careless. I took that criticism for what it was worth as no one really seemed to have lowered their view of me. It was a bittersweet reassurance. I still had good favor with my friends and Elouise still loved me, but now Ariel was gone and I had no doubt Jackson would leap at the chance of her offering herself to him.

But I didn't want to think about that, I wanted to instead make it up to Elouise for what had happened regardless. Our senior year in high school was drawing to a close, and one of the most important nights of our lives was coming up. Prom. And I had no intention of wasting that night. I was going to make so she'd remember that night over the one nearly three years ago.

Chapter 12
Love Everlasting

I woke up pretty early for a day not meant for school. I could hear the sink running in the bathroom that was connected to our bedroom. When I peeked over, I saw Elouise in her hoodie and underwear, leaning over the sink, trying to keep from puking.

It had me exceedingly worried. It'd been weeks since we'd finally graduated from high school. And for the time being, we were taking time for ourselves before going forward with plans for the future. Since we'd been set for life thanks to Elouise and me, we weren't too concerned with work or college. But seeing Elouise at the sink as she was making my mind race. Was it something that I hadn't accounted for? Did she miss something?

I shot out of bed in my shorts and hurried over to Elouise, gently placing my hands on her back, keeping her steady.

"Elle, what's wrong?" I asked, fearful for her.

She shook her head, trying to dismiss whatever worry I had over me.

"Just nauseous," Elouise said calmly. "I'm running diagnostics on my body to make sure it isn't anything major."

I decided to look over her too with my right eye, just for extra measure.

"How long have you been up?" I asked as I scanned her body.

"Only a few minutes. Sorry if I woke you up."

"Don't sweat it. I just wanted to make sure you're alright. It can't be a disease, right? Since you're... Y'know."

"No, at least nothing that bad. It's possible it could've been something ingested."

Food poisoning? Did I do this to her? Oh great, I must've screwed something up during the prep work. Maybe something wasn't clean or something else.

"Gabe, don't worry, it's not something you did," Elouise said, clearly reading my mind as I had gone deathly silent on her mentioning ingesting something harmful. "Even if it was, my body wouldn't have been affected too much by that. It's probably something else."

Yeah... But at that point what else could it have been? If not a major disease, or food poisoning, what could've been the cause for this? And why can't I stop worrying about this? Was I that concerned over a little nausea? Even Elouise was being calm about it all!

Then my right eye came back with a diagnosis: morning sickness caused by...

"Oh my God..." Elouise muttered under her breath as her own body must've given her the same thing.

She stood up and stared at me as I did the same. It was nothing but silence as both of us were trying to figure out what to say. All Elouise could do was shudder with a smile out of excitement. As for me, I had started to grin joyfully.

"Hey, Gabe, you did give me something after all," Elouise joked as she cupped her hands over her mouth as tears began to form under her eyes.

She was pregnant. Of all things, pregnant. But it hadn't been an unsettling shock to us. It was the best thing we could have without knowing we needed it.

I grabbed Elouise and held her so tightly. She began to laugh as she managed to wriggle her arms free to embrace me as well. We laughed with each other in the bathroom, overcome with all manner of emotions that we didn't care about anything else for the time being.

I broke away for a moment to capture her joyous tear streaked face and rested my head on hers.

"Should we tell Jude and Sena?" She asked.

"Screw that, we'll let them figure it out on their own. I want this for us."

"I'm surprised you're not trying to ask how I'm pregnant when I'm a cyborg," Elouise jokingly said through her intermittent laughter.

"I'm not that dumb, besides, you aren't completely machine, I know that for a fact."

"Of course you did. Y'know, when I think about it, this probably happened on prom night."

"That makes sense! I mean, I did try my best to make it the best night you'd ever have yet."

"Well, mission accomplished, Gabe, you got me knocked up!"

More laughter. Yeah, we were probably taking this all too lightly. But as I had stated before, we weren't struggling at all. My Jeep: pretty much paid on the spot. Our home: we only paid utilities at this point. Elouise owned the home from her parents since they never came to see her. Financially, we'd been so rock solid, it'd take a nuclear bomb to ruin our lives, and even then, we would still make it work.

Then my arm began to emit its own special ring whenever someone was calling. It had caught us off-guard so much, we were immediately on edge. What made it worse was the fact the caller was an unknown in my right eye HUD. Meaning it could've been one of three people. Jackson, who I made swear we no longer owed him anything. Ariel, who wasn't our concern anymore, and lastly, Alexander, the man who had assisted in turning our lives into a mess.

I placed my palm to my ear, making a headset, and answered the call.

"Hello Mister Ern," Alexander's familiar grandfatherly voice greeted me. "I hope you are in good health."

"Alexander?" I responded while looking at Elouise, cluing her in on the man I'd been talking to.

Immediately, her face soured over in disgust. She hadn't held Alexander very fondly in her mind. Not only did he help improve on her design that she had put a painstakingly large amount of effort and time into, but he also had turned her body into the cybernetic form she had now.

"Him? Put him on speaker, now!" She demanded.

"I trust Elouise is near you, yes? Would you mind placing me on speaker, I've some information to share with the two of you."

I guess great minds do think alike. I dared not say that aloud, on the off chance Elouise would probably hit me with something non-lethal but extremely painful.

I took the headset off and used my arm's nanomachines to enlarge it into a small speaker device.

"Alright, we can both hear you," I announced to Alexander. "What is it you wanted to tell us?"

"Firstly, I wanted to congratulate the two of you on Elouise's pregnancy."

"How did you—"

"He's been monitoring your body's systems since you were Raven."

Elouise shot me a dirty look, telling me off silently. *And you didn't bother telling me?* She practically shouted through her glare.

"And secondly, I wanted to tell the both of you what will happen to the fetus as it develops inside Elouise's body."

Our faces dropped and we began to stare at the speaker, treating it like Alexander's face.

"Allow me to explain before you begin asking questions. Now, it may trouble you to hear this, but I've been working in this field for a long long time, but no one truly knows about me. The reason being that my methods are not entirely ethical. As for legalities, they hold no sway over me. But in order to continue my work, I need zero human interference. As such my work has made leaps and bounds in secret. You have actually seen a prototype of mine long before we met. Ariel Tessa, otherwise known as Ariel Atlas. Admittedly not my crowning achievement, but she was the inspiration for Elouise, or rather what Elouise will give birth to."

The mention sent shockwaves through my mind about Ariel. All I had learned about her when I helped her in middle school was she was augment by her parents from birth. But when I thought about it now, it made more sense that Alexander had a hand in it. After all, Elouise herself said when I explained why I had helped Ariel then that Atlas had stood little chance against her family's advancements. They were outright inferior and at worst, obsolete. In Ariel's case, she may have been something for them to use, but it was clear when we met again, her parents had been inept at upgrading her.

But, more importantly, what about our baby was going to be so damn special that he had to call?

"Ariel was meant as a test, to see how well my technology would fare in a growing child. Admittedly, Atlas and myself did not see eye to eye, so I had to abandon that venture. Then came you two. Especially Jackson's crude ploy to 'help' the two of you with Elouise's death. I knew you, Gabriel, loved her and would no doubt bring back her true personality. And eventually, conceive your own child. That's why my greatest work to date is not Elouise, but the child inside.

"From the moment the fetus is fully formed, Elouise's body will automatically activate a routine that will augment the body while in the womb. Creating the perfect hybridization of human and machine, without the use of a chaos generator. The device that upgraded your arm and powers Elouise's body. I assure you, the child will be born healthy without complications. I am not without a heart after all."

"Stop it..." Elouise muttered, stricken with horror and disgust. "Stop it now... I don't want this! Can't you stop it?"

She was extremely distraught now. Worse than I'd ever seen. Worse than when I had brutally killed four men to save her. Worse than when I had seen her disown her parents.

"I'm afraid I will not be able to, Miss Gaines; you see, once I had completed my work with you, it was all to be autonomous. No direct involvement by me whatsoever. And once begun, it is impossible to stop. Unless, of course, you opt to not have the child entirely. Which is highly unlikely. Make no mistake, I meant no ill will toward you both, but all the same, I was not letting that halt me in my goals."

Elouise was unable to speak as she slumped to her knees, stunned and horrified. She was completely lost and defeated on what to do next.

"So what happens after? You come in and take the baby?" I asked angrily, potentially seeing Alexander as a new threat. One I wasn't hesitant in killing all the same.

"Nonsense. My work has long been completed. This was, as I've been telling you, merely a courtesy call. Rather you hear from me, instead of making a very disturbing discovery down the line. Having said that."

He ended the call right there and then, not allowing us to even question him for what he had just told us. All that had been left was my anger and Elouise's despair.

I knelt over Elouise, hugging her close as she began to cry softly.

"What're we supposed to do?" She asked, pleading for an answer she couldn't think of.

And the answer was hardly anything good.

"We don't have to say anything about it," I told her outright. She looked at me in shock.

"So what, are we going to lie as well?"

"Not if we're careful," I quickly said. "We'll keep it a secret, but we're going to need help. Which means…"

"Jude and Sena will have to know…"

It wasn't easy. No, it was sickening to us thinking over something like this. But I only wanted the best for our baby. A normal life we had been robbed of. I was sure Elouise wanted that too. But to go so far as to keep this a secret, it was dirty. Worse, we knew, deep down, we'd only be able to keep it a secret for so long until eventually, it was brought to light.

But as the saying goes, we'll cross that bridge when we get there.

"Is everything going to be okay, Gabe?" Elouise anxiously asked.

I hugged her tightly, I didn't tell her what she wanted to hear. But she could feel how determined I was to make everything fine, even as she sobbed into my shoulder from the pain of knowing what was now inevitable. She'd know that I would do anything. I'd done it once before. I may have screwed up here and there, but I never stopped trying.

This was our life. It was marred with death, lies and love. Our baby's life wouldn't be anything like ours. We'd give it the best we could, and then some. Because, for better or worse, this had been all my doing. I was not about to screw this up. Not ever again.